MYCO-TOWN

a magical mushroom fantasy novel

LISA ANN FRANK

Cover design by Jennifer Leigh Selig

EMPRESS
PUBLICATIONS
WWW.EMPRESSPUBLICATIONS.COM

Adina rubella

"We still think in terms of conquest. We haven't become mature enough to think of ourselves as only a tiny part of a vast and incredible universe. Man's attitude toward nature is today critically important because we have now acquired a fateful power to alter and destroy nature. But man is a part of nature and his war against her is inevitably a war against himself. I truly believe this generation must come to terms with nature. We are challenged as humanity has never been challenged before to prove our maturity and our mastery, not of nature, but of ourselves."

—Rachel Carson, author of *Silent Spring*, 1962

Ernest's mask with Witch hazel Jelena

With Gratitude

This book would never exist without the constant encouragement and kind support of the Buckhead Writers Group led by Mark Staufer with insightful guidance.

Thank you, David Freedman, Alex Hoefer, Mick Ryan, Patty Sharaf and Rasheeda Shears for your excellent ideas and for urging me to keep going.

Illicium lanceolatum, a rare Anise

Table of Contents

Philippine lily

Chapter 1 – Philippine Lily

Jill finally gets pregnant late in life. She enters month nine at the hottest time of the year. With all this extra rain, her yard is more jungle than garden with lush growth overflowing the paths.

The tall white Philippine lilies (*Lilium philippinense*) near her front door are doing better than ever. The long, six-inch buds are full of promise, greeting her with their streamlined beauty every time she returns home. Today it seems one bud has doubled in size while she was at yoga class for just one hour. "That's odd," she says out loud, making a mental note to keep her eye on it.

Coming home late the next night from dancing with her rock 'n roll community at Tin Roof Cantina, Jill notices moonlight shining directly on the oversized bud, in perfect alignment. Instead of shining on the smooth exterior, it's radiating a silvery white light from within. The light has an irregular pulse like a flawed, broken heartbeat. She can't believe her eyes.

She wakes up her husband Hank, insisting he come outside to see this in-credible light show for himself. The pulsing light is gone as if it can only be revealed to her.

"For the baby's sake, I know you didn't puff a joint tonight," Hank says, looking her in the eye.

"No way. I'm not making this up."

Jill is now fixated on the strange, otherworldly flower, staring at it from the kitchen window. Tonight, the enchanted lily has grown three times bigger than the other blooms. When she's ready to fall into bed, the flower enlarges again and points toward the moon, ratcheting straight up like a satellite dish tracking a signal. She stares dumbfounded, frightened, mesmerized.

She wants the magic back. When she was that naïve, gullible little girl. When she fell in love the first 10 times. Jill senses the magic is right here in her garden, fantasizing about learning the language of trees, though it would be excruciatingly slow. She yearns to pick up subtle signals from her plants, connected by insects, fed by mycelium underfoot and oxygen ex-changed above.

She stumbles on a new word.
Paragnosis – knowledge obtained only by supernatural means.
Instincts tell her to keep these mysterious messages to herself.
Or will I share these ideas with my unborn child someday?

Two nights later while fast asleep, she jolts awake from a disturbing dream – miniature babies float in glass jars smiling and waving. Jill taps her phone to check the time. It's 3:33 in the morning. She senses an eerie energy in the air. Something is calling her outside.

The super bloom is shaking and swaying its huge white head side to side. Tonight, the glow from inside is a golden warm yellow. Deep buzzing sounds vibrate from within. As if it was waiting for her to witness this

climax, the giant bloom slowly opens wider right before her eyes to release a few flying insects. The humming electric bass sound they're making
turns up the volume.

First 10, then suddenly 100 tiny creatures, then 500 or more explode out
as the impressive blossom, now wide open, shows off its full inner beauty.
The flying creatures seem to be an unusual species of night moth with delicate, pointed iridescent wings. It becomes an endless swarm and a muffled roar.

The moths know exactly where to go. They fly straight up into the tall pine
trees above, about 60 feet. Now the surrounding soil glows with an otherworldly light from roots below the surface. This is a synchronized, choreo-
graphed happening that seems too calculated and visually magnificent to
be real. Jill watches in awe. *No one would even believe me.*

The next morning, the flower is gone without a trace. Every pine needle is
stripped bare from the branches above, transformed into a fine orange
powder, pulsing. It forms a bold spiral curling around the pine trunk like a
barbershop pole, radiating.

Knowing
a lot more than we do.

For the first time, baby Charlie starts kicking.

Chapter 2 – Motherless

J ill and Charlie only have one week together. Mysteriously, Charlie's birth drains her of life.

Weak and pale, she hangs on for those few days, desperate to pass on her unanswered questions and curiosity for nature flowing through her breast milk and her kisses.

Without her feminine influence and wise guidance, her husband Hank and Charlie grow up together more like friends than father and son, raising each other.

Chapter 3 – Growing Up Charlie

At age eight, Charlie's uncombed shiny hair is the color of chipmunk fur, rusty orange and portobello brown. He also has heterochromia – one eye a pale sky blue, the other emerald moss green.

Charlie already knows he's different than the other kids at school. Those boys move fast – running, yelling, punching, competing for soccer balls.

Charlie prefers lying still in one place to let the world unfold in front of him. His pulse can drop as slow as trees grow.

Then, sometimes his heart races at the speed of Earth spinning. Tuning into that fast twirling gives him vertigo. His brain can swirl around so quickly he almost throws up, like speeding on a Six Flags roller coaster, holding on tight. He's learning not to go that deep for his own protection.

He loves watching bold red Cardinals
swoop through secret tunnels
they find between conifer limbs in the collection of rare plants
he inherited from Jill.

He listens intently to hawks screeching high above.
Riding wind currents without moving a feather.
These are the rhythms that matter, not the horseplay those other boys live for. He wonders if they'll ever change and learn to honor nature. Or will they grow up to be self-centered, short-term thinkers who gobble up nature's resources instead of treasuring them?

As Charlie's mind sharpens, Hank dulls his with alcohol – self-medicating and numbing his heart to push away the loneliness. *Jill would know how to encourage Charlie. But she's not here, so I have to keep trying without her. Man, do I miss her tonight.*

With fewer photography assignments coming in, Hank hasn't shaved all week. He starts drinking earlier in the day. Charlie sees his dad unraveling and he worries.

*   *   *

Legs stretched out in the shape of an Egyptian pyramid, Charlie lies in the grass on his back staring straight up into the clouds.

He imagines every vertebra in his spine growing delicate roots pushing through his skin,
gently connecting to the red clay below,
reaching out in all directions.
Making connections.
Sharing nutrients.
Sharing love secrets.

He's a natural daydreamer – able to wander his mind with the wind,
follow subtle moves wispy clouds make
expanding so slowly their upward drift is barely perceptible.
But Charlie perceives it,
drinking in nature's details like mother's milk.

Across the boundary of Charlie's lot is a swing set in the yard that backs up to his. A girl his age swings alone; they're separated by a black, wrought iron fence. Her long, strawberry-blonde braid reaches down her back. She's feeling empowered in her silver glittery shoes, using her rich imagination to become an enchanted princess swinging on vines.

They've watched each other before. Today, she watches him more closely.

As Charlie lies in the grass, native plants most people would call weeds begin to jump up around his body, stretching six feet above the lawn.

What am I seeing? Ella wonders to herself. *Is he making the grass grow?*

She's drawn to the boy and wants a closer look, so she sneaks into his yard through a hole in the fence.

"Can you do that to me?"

Startled out of his daydream, Charlie sits up, instantly sensing the girl is familiar and safe, so he says, "OK. Let's try."

Ella lays down beside him and waits. Soon the grass starts growing taller around them both as if their combined energies accelerate the action. Charlie's powers are fortified by hers.

The tall stalks begin to flower with Aster-like yellow, white, and lavender blossoms opening eight feet above their heads. They're surrounded by the fresh green growth towering over their fresh naïve faces. The scent is delicious – like Juicy Fruit gum.

"Who are you?" the girl asks.

"I'm Charlie. I live here. Who are you?"

"I'm Ella. I live there. How do you make the grass grow so fast?"

"I think Mother Nature likes me."

Ella reaches for his hand and holds it tight, something she's never done before. It's a first for Charlie too. He's rarely felt the warmth of hand touching hand like this. If Jill were alive, she would hold his hand every day.

Tingling energy tickles through them and it feels so right. Ella gives in to the feeling.

As they look up at the instant garden they've grown together, two tiny Brown-headed Nuthatches land in the new stalks, making them sway. They're a couple. Though Charlie can't speak their language yet, the pair is telling Charlie and Ella they too can form a lifelong bond.

Brown-headed Nuthatches are social birds. Moving to a nearby Camellia branch, the birds sit side-by-side and reach over to preen each other's feathers. Believing in each other. Trusting each other.

"Did you call those birds to come closer?" Charlie asks.

"I was thinking about birds but didn't know any would really come," Ella says, smiling even bigger.

These unforgettable moments will imprint a love of nature on both children, fueling a lifelong quest to understand how nature works.

That's when Hank calls out from the screened porch. "Charlie, lunch is ready. Come and get it while it's hot."

"I have to go. But I'm glad I met you, Ella. Maybe we can play another nature game sometime."

She watches his every step as he walks away toward the house, feeling a fluttering in her chest she's never felt before. *Please don't go . . .*

There's some close connection with this gentle boy she doesn't understand.
It's sensual though she can't grasp what that even means.
It's a physical burning in her center.
It's emotional.
He pulls her in like an irresistible whirlpool of longing
that can follow you throughout your life.

Charlie feels an unfinished longing too. He's disappointed he couldn't stay with her today. He thinks to himself, *I'm probably more comfortable with plants and trees, wild birds and Bumble bees anyway. How could this little girl ever understand me?*

That's the only time their paths cross. Walking to Nancy Creek a week later, he sees a huge moving van in front of her house, loading up couches and heavy boxes. Ella's father is promoted to president of the Baltimore office of his accounting firm and must move there. The two would-be friends may never meet again.

*   *   *

Elementary school years roll by. Charlie still keeps to himself – certain he's destined to be a loner. He's sustained by an inherent talent for gardening, caring for hundreds of plants Jill left behind. Speaking their language, reading the signs for when they need water or food. He becomes an expert horticulturist and mycologist, all self-taught.

Charlie keeps the collection alive, using it as a living sanctuary and laboratory for his mushroom experiments.

It's a real comfort to Hank since he finds the garden overwhelming. He's in awe of Charlie for knowing what to do.

While transplanting a clump of the perennial shade plant Epimedium that's outgrowing its original space, Charlie's fascinated by the pure white lacy fungal threads tightly packed through the damp dark soil. He sees patterns the underground mycelium trace, eager to introduce and connect plant roots to each other, making love matches.
Encouraging them to knit together and communicate.
Pushing their white fingertips into the rich, brown-skinned soil.
As close as kissing.

Days later in his science class, Charlie's teacher shows a diagram of internal systems that fuel the human body. He sees the same lacy threads of neural networks lighting up the brain, pumping oxygen and nutrients from head to toe. They look and act like the fungal roots he found underground in his garden.

The visual parallel is thrilling. His mind takes off into another daydream. Imagining hot energy pulsing through mycelium in the soil and through his own body's internal systems. It's a life-changing epiphany for the young boy who loves nature and science. He usually overthinks every word before he says anything in class. Today, Charlie is emboldened to speak up about his revelation.

"Those hairy threads of neurons in the brain look like the hairy threads of mushrooms that attach to tree roots," he tells his teacher, Mr. Holtby. "Both networks must be communicating the same way." Years later, Charlie will learn fungi have more DNA in common with people and animals than with plants. Maybe Charlie is more mycelium than man.

The brazen class bully, Liam, snaps back. "Hairy roots? *You're* a hairy freak! What the hell are you talking about?"

"Liam! That's enough. Charlie makes a very good point," Mr. Holtby says in Charlie's defense. "Nature's patterns *do* repeat in hundreds of ways. This is an excellent example."

But the damage is done. Charlie's face is burning red. His exhilarating moment of discovery is smashed to pieces by embarrassment. It will take years before Charlie finds the confidence to ever speak up in class again. He wants to hurt Liam back.

So, he dreams up a little plot for revenge. He selects a spider in his garden that packs a mild touch of poisonous venom and asks it to crawl into an empty matchbox.

Before releasing the spider at school, Charlie whispers to the tiny, light green creature, "That's the boy I want you to bite," placing the open box behind Liam's chair. Liam doesn't feel a thing as the delicate spider climbs up the bully's body and plunges its venom into his upper lip.

But something goes wrong. The next day, everyone learns Liam is in the hospital. The word at school is he almost died. Charlie's plan backfires and he's terrified. This was not Charlie's intent. The poison must have been too strong.

Finally, Liam returns to school two weeks later. His upper lip is still swollen, badly making him look like a monster. For the next few weeks, Charlie lurks behind corners, trying to stay invisible as he slinks away to keep out of Liam's sight. Liam can never know he was involved.

It's a heavy burden to keep the secret to himself. And a powerful lesson to realize his connections to nature can have destructive, maybe fatal consequences.

Overnight, the transplanted Epimedium triples in size – growing as if it were in the ground for three or four years. Though this has happened before, Charlie is amazed, baffled. It's still hard to admit he has something to do with it.

*   *   *

Hank and his buddy Phillip are enjoying a bottle of wine on the screened porch with its elevated view of the garden.

They bonded almost 20 years ago over a Sonny Emory drum solo that blew their minds and blew the roof off the jazz club in Sandy Springs. Since then, both friends married and became fathers. Phillip has two sons; Hank has Charlie. They still make an effort to keep in touch.

Hank trusts Phillip and tonight he needs to talk.

Hank is thinking: *"Sometimes Charlie scares me with his uncanny abilities to tune in to nature. It's like he's half boy, half plant. Part bird, part kid. Part tree, living at his own pace in some other dimension."*

Hank says: "How are your boys doing?"

Phillip is thinking: *"I wish my boys were into nature like Charlie. But they're addicted to the Xbox and their damn phones. I can't even get them to go outside for a hike or throw a football around."*

Phillip says: "They're doin' great. Really getting good with computers."

Hank is thinking: *"Feels like I'm only half a man without Jill. I'm at a loss about how to give Charlie the support he needs to pursue his passions that are showing up at such an early age."*

Hank says: "Can you believe how fast kids change? Charlie understands more about the world around him every week."

Hank refills their glasses with Cabernet. Hahn Estates. Monterey, California. $12 a bottle.

He buys four bottles at a time now; he used to buy two. It masks the grief. Soothes the sad emptiness without her kisses.

"That's all good stuff, Hankster," Phillip says. "Let the kid find his way. Let Charlie be Charlie and just enjoy it."

"You're right. Thanks." Hank says.

Hank is thinking: *"Phillip gets how hard this is."*

Hank pours another, breathing a little easier. Hahn Estates. Monterey, California. $12 a bottle.

"Is it Tuesday or Wednesday night? I lost track," Hank asks in a stupor.

Phillip watches his old friend sinking further. He can tell Hank needs a distraction, needs to get out of the house.

"Let's catch some jazz at Café 290 next week. I'll text you."

Chapter 4 – Rendezvous

Ella flourishes in Baltimore and Washington, DC, moving to both cities for her father's work. As an only child, she evolves to become an independent, self-assured city girl, streetwise and confident. Mature beyond her 18 years.

She grows almost too close to her father Martin. Though she tries to hang out with boys her age, they never measure up to Martin's interesting stories and perspectives.

He's a rare accountant who loves freeform jams in intimate jazz clubs, especially keyboardists. Since Ella was 12, he brings her along as his date even though she's underage. He wants her to experience world-class music for herself. His wife Theresa isn't interested in loud music or crowded places. For Ella, it's thrilling to be the only kid in the dark, sultry clubs, sheltered by her dad's warm chest.

One family story that sticks with her is the night Martin's father took him to the Rainbow Room when *he* was a kid in Manhattan in the '60s. The headliner was legendary jazz pianist Earl "Fatha" Hines. Ella's grandfather had a few too many whiskies that night, and in the middle of a song, ran up to the stage with his hand outstretched to greet Hines and show his appreciation. Young Martin cringed with embarrassment when Hines ignored his dad and kept on playing. He had to slink back to his seat – his fantasy unrealized.

Ella knows Martin's fantasy is to play jazz piano himself, but he could never quite take that leap. He's also a realist – choosing the safe route as a corporate accountant, making a good living he can count on. He's not reckless enough to improvise and flow like a sax solo. The uncertainties of a musician's life would be too stressful. He only lets his artistic side shine with his daughter.

*   *   *

Ella's family moves around the northeast, appeasing Martin's constant need for a change of scene, as if moving cancels out the monotony of spreadsheets.

Theresa has had enough. She puts her foot down, making it clear she's ready to move back home. Her aging parents in Atlanta need her. Her husband promised they would eventually return south once Ella grew up.

Martin gives in. He's able to secure one last job transfer as a senior vice president in the Buckhead office. Ella's first reaction is disappointment.

"I don't want to go back to such a conservative place, especially for my last year of high school," she says, whining.

"Atlanta has changed since we lived there," Martin tells Ella. "It's much hipper now. And you always loved the trees."

One morning while lathering her thick rust-colored hair in the shower, a flashback pierces her memory. Her last image of Atlanta is meeting that nature boy who lived in a garden forest behind her house. *Was his name Charlie? Is he still there?*

Even though they met so briefly, she never forgot the combustible connection that immediately sparked between them. *Was he my first crush? Is he the reason fate brings me back to my hometown? Could I ever find him again? I'd like to . . .*

*   *   *

Hank notices Charlie isn't himself. The usually cheerful kid now has frequent moods of dark blue despair after his spider prank went awry.

As Charlie grows taller and wiser, Hank senses a distance between them. As if they come from different roots.

"I know you're sensitive, Charlie," Hank says, pouring another big splash of Cabernet. "You inherited an appreciation for Mother Nature from your mother. She would understand what you're going through, maybe better than I can." His father tells him, "I still miss her every day," which only adds to Charlie's sadness.

Hank goes on. "She wrote a bunch of personal journals over the years. I've been saving them for you. I think now is the right time for you to read them. Maybe some of her ideas in those notebooks can help you make sense of things."

Jill's journals

When Charlie returns from school the next day, a large pile of mismatched books is stacked on his bed.

Jill, inspired by reading the diaries of Anne Frank and Anaïs Nin at an early age, left behind an extensive collection of diaries and collages spanning almost four decades. Charlie savors the hand-written books in segments, hoping for clues to understand the quirky woman who loved plants and natural phenomena like he does — since he'll never know her in person. Her journals are the closest thing to hearing her voice.

Pages and pages of his mother's random thoughts never read before by anyone but her.

Or did she know all along she was writing these journals for her unborn son?

*   *   *

Charlie is walking the trails at the Blue Heron Nature Preserve a few blocks from his house this chilly wet January morning. The urban park covers 30 acres in three connected parcels. By coincidence, Charlie and Hank's property sits in between the three sites, serving as another arm of the protected nature corridor the Blue Heron staff nurtures for birds, beavers, amphibians, fox and other creatures, ensuring they'll have safe cover and food. Charlie's garden certainly provides that.

Blue Heron maintains four beehives to help protect the endangered Honey bee. Since Honey bees only travel within a four-mile radius, they love stopping in at Charlie's place where they encounter a four-season buffet of gourmet flowering trees, shrubs and perennials found nowhere else. Charlie likes to imagine the pollen they gather here adds an extra spiciness and complexity to their honey.

*   *   *

It's been raining for days – soaking the soil, quenching the deepest tree roots and activating miles of mycelium feeding the subterranean network. The paths feel spongey, bouncing with her steps as Ella explores the nature preserve that didn't exist as a protected park when she lived here.

The air is so moist and clean, she tells herself, confirming Atlanta's tree canopy is unusual for such a big city. Pockets of forest like this still exist because Atlanta developed so recently compared to the paved-over northeastern cities she's used to. *Maybe living here won't be so bad.*

She hears rustling in the shrubs along Nancy Creek. Suddenly a furry fat humpy shape waddles a few feet in front of her. *Oh my God, it's a beaver,* she says under her breath. *I'm not believing this.*

As she turns her focus to its extraordinary flat paddled tail, she trips on a camouflaged tree root thrusting into the path. In an instant, her left ankle twists and she's on the ground.

That's when Charlie walks her way from the other direction, seeing her topple over. There's an instant recognition even before they speak.

"I twisted my ankle on that root and I'm having trouble getting up."

"Put your arm around my neck and see if you can stand," Charlie says.

A magnetic current surges when they touch. His stomach feels like crickets are hopping inside his gut. She can't stop smiling, her heart pounding.

"I *know* you," Ella says. "Those *eyes.*" *One blue. One green.*
"Didn't we meet as kids when I lived near here?"

"You're Ella."

"Are you Charlie?"

Their eyes lock. No more words come. It's a heart-to-heartbeat connection that rocks their equilibrium.

Feeling like the intensity is too much to handle, he finally says, "Let's see if your foot is broken."

He concentrates, intentionally lowering his body temperature to make his fingers ice cold. He's learned to manage his powers since they last met, when together they made native grasses grow high above their heads.

His freezing cold fingers and palms scan her foot, as if reaching below the skin, between every muscle and bone. He channels a healing flow of energy to the bruised places. She relaxes, surrendering to his touch.

The swelling starts to disappear before her eyes. She can hardly feel the pain. As if his caress soothes it away.

"It doesn't hurt anymore. What did you do?" she asks, amazed.

Charlie looks her in the eye and smiles. "I can't believe we've met again."

"I think that beaver deliberately tripped me up to bring us together," Ella says, laughing.

Two tiny Brown-headed Nuthatches – now endangered from habitat loss – land on a Beech branch overhead. Descendants of the original pair, they're here to confirm these two humans belong together – and in Georgia. The birds sense that over time, Charlie and Ella will build something important, something that moves civilization forward.

A swarm of Honey bees swoops in. Their loud humming buzz is full of life, like live rock 'n roll coaxing you to get up and dance. They fly close to Ella's cheeks, swirling in rounded shapes that look like mushrooms.

Drips of honey fall from their wings onto Ella's lips – sticky and delicious. She wants to kiss him but holds back. *Not so soon. Savor it. Drink in this incredible moment,* she tells herself, still reeling from the shock of finding him again so easily. Like 50 kittens purring, the buzzing hum soothes and welcomes her to Charlie's world.

She realizes the cadence and rhythm of their humming is similar to the melody of Billie Holiday's *You Go to My Head.* Her Dad taught her the song when they frequented The Hamilton Live, one of DC's best jazz clubs. She's loved it ever since.

The bees hum the song.

And then she kisses him.

Chapter 5 – Charlie Blooming

I t's the end of August and Charlie turns 20 this week. His torso grows even taller today, still developing in body and brain. Atlanta remains the last big city in the U.S. that still has pockets of old-growth forest and the thickest tree canopy of any other large American city. But destructive development is everywhere. He feels pain and gloom every time a nearby residential lot is scraped bare to make way for another giant McMansion. Chipping away at the priceless tree cover that could solve so many issues connected to climate change.

The new McMansion people don't see the value in the natural buffers of native trees and shrubs they're eliminating. But Charlie gets it. He knows every mature tree taken down impacts dozens of trees around it and millions of insects, bird nests, butterfly cocoons, bat habitats, invisible bacteria and connective mycelium below, snake dens and hundreds more pieces making up the complex natural puzzle quilt.

Hank and Charlie still live in the aging ranch house Jill bought in a little-known part of Buckhead back in 1987. She was there for three years before the Georgia 400 highway came barreling right through the middle of their neighborhood to connect the outer suburbs with the inner city. 40,000 mature trees were bulldozed to clear its path.

Jill's journal shows she tried to appeal to the road builders' common sense. There's even a newspaper clipping with a photo of her in a group of protesters holding a sign that reads *MASS TRANSIT IS THE ANSWER.*

Georgia 400: Gateway to north Atlanta

PROTEST

JOEY IVANSCO / Staff

Department of Transportation officials confront a group of demonstrators near the toll-booth plaza before opening ceremonies for the Georgia 400 extension.

Newspaper clipping

Jill's journal - November 18, 1988

The city asked for comments on building Georgia 400 in our neighborhood. I stepped up to the dark, rickety stage in the old church where they were recording people's opinions even though I knew it was a futile exercise. None of our comments would be considered, especially mine. I'm sure I was the only one to speak up for the wildlife. "How many foxes, coyotes, owls, chipmunks, bluebirds and so many others will be displaced when all those trees are removed?" I asked. Somebody on the planning team has to care. Yet I knew they didn't. I imagine the guy recording me saying to himself, "This hippie girl lives in the past. We can't let a few raccoons and squirrels in the way of progress." I'm glad I did it, even if it felt hopeless.

22

Like all the unanswered letters I've written to mayors, city councils and developers about saving trees.

They never listened. The eight-lane highway was excavated and built deep below street level. The asphalt slab carries thousands of cars and trucks every day, erasing the forest, spewing CO_2. And destroying the valuable services trees freely give to clean the air, water and promote wellness.

Yet Jill left a small legacy of her own on her half-acre lot. Thanks to Grover, a favorite former boyfriend who worked with her at the Atlanta Botanical Garden, they planted almost 200 species of rare trees, shrubs and perennials on her property – castoffs and surplus the botanical garden would never use.

The house is the last holdout from the original neighborhood built in the '50s, the only ranch house still standing. Thirty-five years after Grover started planting his tiny saplings, the house is completely hidden from the street, screened by uncommon hollies, mature hemlocks and other conifers, little-known trees like *Katsura, Parrotia*, an evergreen *Kousa dogwood* and a *Sinojackia* covered in snow white, bell-shaped flowers every April.

The property is surrounded by million-dollar McMansions owned by people with small lawns soaked in pesticides, manicured and clipped, all the same. Hank and Charlie's place is natural and wild, rich with character. Neighbors look the other way.

Jill's journals speak about learning the language of nature. She's certain her trees, wild birds, spiders and the whole symphony of life are communicating with each other. She wants in on it. Charlie feels it too, decoding, uncovering, tuning in.

December 11, 1998
Found this Chinese proverb:
> *The best time to plant a tree is 20 years ago.*
> *The second best time is now!*

May 23, 2008
Scientists are proving trees live in harmony, collaborating with each other
to share the wealth with their neighbors. Their method: attaching delicate
roots to fragile fingers of mushroom mycelium to secure the connection,
wired together like golden threads of a silk tapestry joining hands. Trans-
ferring water, essential nutrients and encouragement. One teaspoon of
forest soil contains several miles of fungal filaments. Incredible. The soil is
loaded with electrical wiring that benefits the entire clan, even sharing
with other tree species, not just their own.

What if human societies could function like this? We did once when we
lived in small villages. One bison killed fed young and old for days, using
every morsel. Everyone was taken care of by caring for each other, collabo-
rating.

*   *   *

The private garden is an endless source of entertainment for the gentle,
observant young man. He watches a huge furry black and yellow Bumble bee trying to balance on a fragile Epimedium blossom. The magenta
flower can barely hold the weight of the big fat bee.

Yet Charlie knows the two are having an intimate conversation. Hovering
over the scene with Jill's antique magnifying glass, he can feel the furry
black legs tickling the purple flower's innards in just the right spot, making
her laugh and shudder with orgasmic chills. Sensual thrills.

The bee's probing makes the flower relax and let go all the way to release
her succulent nectar and powdery pollen, sticking to the bumbler's hairy
legs. It's all part of a larger design. They seem to be dancing for the fun of
it, but Charlie senses a life-and-death purpose too. The flower, the bee
and Charlie are all laughing together. All three need each other.

Charlie asks a couple of Bumble bees to call their friends and fellow dancers to form a circle spinning above his head. He sticks his hand right into
the center with fingers outstretched, not touching the vibrating, humming

dancers, a mix of orange and black Monarch butterflies, several species of Bumble bees and yellow and black Swallowtail butterflies. His arm lights up with an x-ray image of capillaries and veins pushing silvery juices up and down his long, elegant arm. The connection is communicated.

One of Charlie's 18 Epimediums

Charlie has a special affinity for birds. While the youngest student to take the Audubon Society's Master Birder course, the teacher describes the screeching call of the Red-tailed hawk phonetically. "The hawk's call sounds like *Creee, creee.*"

Charlie hears something more. He closes his eyes and listens deeply. He hears anguish in their crying voices. He hears, *"Seeee me. Help me. Feeeel me. Help me."* Clues about a collapsing ecosystem grasping for a way to re-bound.

Though bird populations are dwindling fast because the tallest trees keep disappearing for new human homes, he still encounters owls, six species of woodpeckers, graceful Blue herons and many others in his garden. Yet it's the hummingbirds who attract him most. He considers the tiny, hyper-sensitive creatures his closest friends.

Every spring, when they return from Mexico after flying 600 miles to reach Georgia to nest, Charlie feels whole again.

When they leave every fall, racing against winter's chill, his mood sinks, dreading their exit.

Chapter 6 – Grover

Jill's journal - November 5, 2007:
Why does he have to be so stubborn? Why can't we be friends? This deep hole in my heart still aches when I can't pick up the phone to say hello or ask him a plant question. It's Grover's birthday and I'm missing him so much today. And every day. I made the excruciating choice to leave him for Hank. Was it a mistake? With Hank in my life, Grover stays away. He wouldn't even come to the wedding, of course. Wish he could see how the garden is maturing. But he knows.

I'll never forget when he planted the one-gallon Daphniphyllum. "This will soften the hard corner of the house," he said. I'm thinking, yeah right. That little thing? Today the tree fills the entire space, reaching above the two-story roofline, engulfing the brick edge and everything around it, just as he imagined. That's when I realized horticulturists can see into the future. They know what each plant will become, visualizing 5, 10, 25 years ahead, seeing in their mind how a tree or shrub will grow into the space they've chosen for it. Since G had access to the rare, evergreen tree before anyone else, I like to think it's the biggest most mature Daphniphyllum specimen in Atlanta.

*   *   *

Daphniphyllum flower

Hank is not the kind of guy who gets his hands dirty. As an architectural photographer with an artistic eye, he needs total control of his environment, more comfortable with digital imagery on computers than caring for living plants. The dense landscape even became too much for Jill to handle by herself. Thankfully, Charlie knows what to do. Hank's mind wanders for a minute, regretting that Jill never had the chance to garden together with their beautiful son. *She would marvel at how Charlie takes to gardening so naturally.*

"Why are there so many different Epimediums in Mom's garden?" Charlie asks his dad one night. "Was that her favorite flower?"

"I'm not sure, son." Hank doesn't even know which plant that is. Actually, it was Grover's favorite flower. He shrewdly collected 18 varieties from small specialty nurseries and by mail order before the Internet. Their flowers are delicate, subtle, anything but showy, and yet complex. Like him.

"Tell me more about Mom when you first met her."

Hank tries to find the words. "There was this chemistry between us we couldn't ignore. She was the writer for the Midtown Business Association. I was their photographer. I think you know she was living with Grover, the guy who planted the garden. Though she wasn't available, I couldn't get her out of my mind because she was passionate, enthusiastic and so alive. We were both turning 40 that year and thought that was so old. We were sure if we didn't act on the strong attraction, it might never come again. We were determined to rearrange our lives so we could be together. We were married a year later."

Epimedium pseudoacuminatum, another one of 18 species in Charlie's garden

"How did you know she was the one for you? How did Mom know you were the right one for her?" Now that Charlie is reunited with Ella, these are the same questions he asks himself. *Is Ella the right one for me?*

"It's hard to explain, Charlie. I felt an energy in my bones telling me I'd met my match."

That's exactly how Charlie feels about Ella yet he's too timid to say it out loud to his dad.

Charlie looks so familiar to Hank right now – a younger version of someone he knows. But who? It hits him later that night as he's falling asleep. Charlie looks a lot like Grover and has his sensibilities. How is that possible?

For the first time, Hank admits to himself his son doesn't look like him at all. *Why is this kid six inches taller than I am? Like Grover. Did the master horticulturist somehow plant his seed in Jill's womb remotely without physical contact? Can this explain some of the other unexplainable visions Jill had right before she died?* Hank gets a nauseous, gnawing feeling in his stomach. The edgy tingling starts spreading through his body. *No, no. It can't be possible.*

*   *   *

Back in 1990, Grover and Jill both worked at the Atlanta Botanical Garden when it was young, nothing like the flashy, expensive destination it is today. The small staff joked there were two kinds of workers – inside people and outside people. The outside people who worked hard in the brutal heat, humidity and freezing cold, physically maintained the gardens, resenting the inside people who worked in air-conditioned and heated offices, never sweating or freezing in the elements.

Grover was the superintendent of grounds outside. Jill was the garden's first PR director inside. She got to know him while writing a brochure for a symposium on Georgia perennials. Jill wanted a catchy title for his lecture – *Learning to Speak the Language of Plants.* A bit gimmicky and not his style, Grover agreed to it anyway. And a prescient harbinger of her own obsession in the end.

Though Jill was outgoing, and Grover was a man of few words, they grew together anyway. It seemed wise to keep their romance a secret from the rest of the staff, adding another element of danger and sizzle.

Black plastic pots of rare tree seedlings and other collectible plants started lining up on Jill's driveway since Grover had no other place to keep them. They were the extra castoffs the Botanical Garden had no place for. To keep them alive, he had to water the pots often which was getting old. He finally planted a Shasta viburnum in her front lawn. That started it all.

Without a plan or design of any kind, he began transforming her neglected landscape, creating planting beds by amending the hard, red clay with aged horse manure from nearby stables at Chastain Park. The root-bound pots started disappearing from the driveway; their contents finding homes in the ground.

Jill learned the botanical names as she worked beside him weeding and watching. The lifelong recordkeeper started a garden journal. There's a page for every day of the year to document what was blooming when. Notes were added by year, so several pages have multiple entries, making it easy to compare bloom times from one year to another. By the time Charlie starts reading the garden journals, there are 14 years of data.

Sometimes her notes are purely factual. Sometimes they are poetry. As the years pass, she observes more closely, searching for meaning.

Jill's garden journal - April 21, 1995:
Styrax loaded with buds. Two flowers open. Thousands of perfectly round white buds hang heavy like musical notes in slanted rows. Ascending. Descending.

Charlie takes her cue literally. He listens for harmonies and musical riffs the *Styrax* buds are emitting and hears them loud and clear. Neighboring plants become the tree's audience too, picking up on a tinkling and clanging beat people cannot hear. When it's windy, the tall pines dance and sway to the silent xylophone music.

April 22, 1999:
Mahonia berries ripen to anthocyanin-rich juicy stain. Would a Mahonia wine bring a special healthful buzz – prickly and rich in a deep purple tonic?

This entry prompts Charlie to research medicinal tinctures and brews from berries, mushrooms, seeds and flowers. Somehow by instinct, he taps into centuries of knowledge passed from generation to generation thousands of years old. The homemade drinks sharpen his brain and enhance his sight from within. His mysterious powers are gradually building, developing.

Drinking his potions, Charlie feels a kinship with Cherokee medicine men who once lived on the same land. Maybe he was born in the wrong time, better suited to a simpler, low-tech society that flourished here 500 years ago.

July 5, 1999: First Adina rubella globes floating full. Tiny planets pierced by whiskers of celestial filaments. Sputnik spacecraft orbiting the planet.

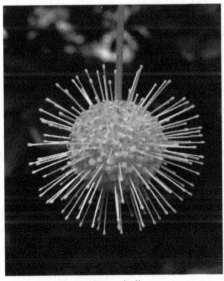

Adina rubella

July 14, 2000: Large Eucomis flower two-thirds open. Streamlined green praying mantis (3" long) hanging off the flower's tip with arms dangling down like a carved female figurehead on the front of a pirate ship except looking down. I tickled its antenna and entire body quivered.

April 22, 2001: Orange Trumpet vine looking good. First burgundy Columbine opens. Second large purple Iris opens; the most complex pattern of yellow and purple of any other flower. Curving ridged yellow paths guide insects straight to the delicious center like stripes on a highway or bowling alley floor. A yellow brick road.

April 24, 1994: First hummingbird returns.

A clue for Charlie to be on the lookout for them in late April every year.

July 30, 2003: A record 11 flower stalks stand tall on Cimicifuga in tight bud taking forever to open. "The sign of a truly elegant plant," Mr. Grover believes.

August 12, 2001: Huge hawk perched outside office window in full view for 20 min; spotted chest, intense dark eyes, henna orange strong back. What a gift to be so close for that long.

September 5, 2005: Pink Begonia peaking under bathroom window. Like elegant jewelry for feminine fairies – seed and flower dangling together on arching, ruby red stems.

September 20, 2006: For weeks I've enjoyed her gorgeous 2" yellow and black body suspended above the Symphytum and Maclaya, hanging right in the center of her distinctive web with white zig zag zipper shape. But today my zipper spider (Arigope aurantia) is gone. Miss her!

The garden journals help Charlie learn the botanical names and when to expect their blooms.

Chapter 7 – Jill's Journals

Charlie and Ella never forgot each other though they couldn't imagine they'd meet so many years later. *In the back of my mind, you were always right there but more like a ghost or spirit than a real person,* Charlie tells himself.

They're spending more time together, hiking in nature, listening to music. But cautiously. There's something so strong between them, with a sense this is meant to be, that they both want to go slow for fear of losing each other again or blowing it up too fast.

Ella notices the stack of Jill's journals in Charlie's bedroom. "You're welcome to read them," he says. She sees right away how special they are. No two books are alike. Jill evidently collected blank books of different sizes and time periods, many from garage sales. Every page is filled with her handwritten scrawl edge to edge, page after page. "It's like she's right here talking to us," Ella says.

June 2, 2012:
Tin Roof scene moves to a deeper degree last night. I danced a lot, every time with Willy – a first. We're getting closer. Outside, I told Fred, "This guy is a great dancer, but I really like his brain." W told me again how aware he's always been of the destructive nature of advertising, "a relatively new invention."

W: "I like everything about you," inspecting my outfit. "I bet you'd look great naked too."

J: "Well you'll never know . . . ." I back away smiling large.

Even tho we're both married to others, I still want to know him. I've learned a lot from him about not needing another person, especially someone unavailable. Move on to flirt, dance, hug others. But don't let your heart open too far and shatter. Yet we always come back to each other. A pattern I hope will last our lifetimes, even if other partners lock in. I want him as a special friend.

Sometimes Charlie finds her journals too personal. Crazy stories about her old boyfriends, current friends and the rock 'n roll dancing club where she's a regular every week. When his mom writes about other men like this, Charlie gets uncomfortable and closes the book.

"Those are the good parts," Ella smiles.

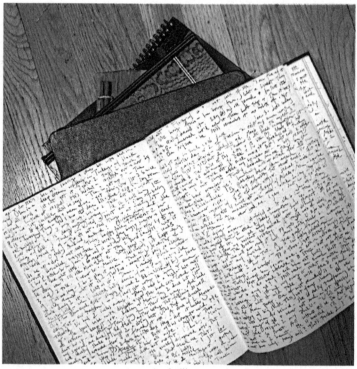

A stack of Jill's journals

Chapter 8 – Fungal Queendom

Jill's journal – October 6, 2006:
Rogue mushroom freaks at Radical Mycology.com call the underworld of mycelium the Fungal Queendom. The words resonate so well together. If only the term could ever become mainstream and revered – a new religion.

Queendom implies elegant matriarchs, wise and efficient. Contrast that with Kingdom which implies testosterone, greed and war. Feminine energy wants to live in harmony with nature, not destroy it for short-term profits like the men. Mushrooms are other worldly, superior to most life forms in so many ways – the glue that strings the planet together from the underside out. Their DNA is closer to humans than plants, though evolving millions of years longer than humans.

Radical Mycology becomes one of Charlie's favorite sites. He's fascinated by mushrooms' ability to absorb toxins in water and soil. With so much polluted storm water run-off, dirty air and contaminated creeks around him, Charlie quietly experiments with natural ways to counteract the damage.

Developers keep getting permits to upset the natural balance in his once-wooded neighborhood. It baffles him how so few speak up to stop them. He can't bear to look anymore as bulldozers push over mature pines, magnolias, poplars and oaks. Charlie understands the inter-connections between them. How their roots are linked by delicate strands of fungi, feeding each other. The destroyers don't even consider these interdependent love relationships. Their backwards, uninformed thinking makes him want to retreat, finding friendships with trees and birds more satisfying than with *Homo sapiens.*

* * *

Cultivating mushrooms in the wild can be tricky. Soil conditions must be exactly right. Moisture levels, light levels and host trees' chemistries must align. But Charlie has a special knack for making things grow. Along the shaded banks of Nancy Creek, he inoculates rotting logs with mushroom spores in unlikely combinations.

He's read ants and termites actively cultivate mushrooms in mysterious ways that mycologists don't understand. But he does understand. As their nests break down rotting logs and enrich the soil, he uses his special powers of concentration to accelerate the process. Charlie plays with this delicate interdependency of insect and fungus as if motivating two lovers to achieve lift-off.

Pumpkin orange Chanterelles are spreading quickly near the road. Deadly white Amanitas are taking over along the water's edge. He ordered a rare fungus from Hawaii that's doing surprisingly well, its fruits in the shape of outstretched fingers in dusty pale pink with lavender bumps.

For three years, Charlie and the same petite Ruby-Throated Hummingbird have flirted and bonded. The hyper little jewel guides him to her nest to show off her miraculous handiwork. The intricate cup is held together with fine white spider silk woven throughout the soft bed. Other threads of silk anchor it to the Daphniphyllum branch. The proud mother is completely comfortable having Charlie nearby for the next three weeks closely watching two babies hatch, feed, then grow strong enough to fly.

Now that it's summer, she makes it clear she wants to communicate with Charlie by the way she hovers around his nose, looking straight into his eyes. Her pulsing body sounds like a mouth harp buzzing and purring louder as she comes closer. Swooping up and down. Left then right.

He senses she speaks some primeval language he may be able to decipher, a language she's urging him to learn. If only he can shed his doubts and reasons why it's impossible. Because it *is* possible. She needs him to understand her. She needs him on her side.

* * *

Gene Jenkins has worked with Chemlawn for 19 years. For the last nine, his territory is Buckhead which is one hell of a commute from his place in Douglasville. He's benefited from the changes as older homes are demolished for rambling McMansions, increasing demand for spraying pesticides on newly planted lawns.

When he started here, the lots had plenty of woods and smaller lawns. People didn't care if weeds punctuated them. But these nouveau riche homeowners clear every native tree and shrub, making way for the largest house possible. Remaining space in front and back is covered with golf course green sod in geometric squares and needs treatments twice a month to keep Georgia's vigorous weeds and trees from taking root. He's also a pro at spraying toxic Roundup along the edges and sidewalk cracks, so every client's property is weed-free and clear.

Most people think those bright green lawns are beautiful. To Charlie, it's the opposite. They're ugly and phony, going against how nature works, killing beneficial insects and upsetting the balance. A waste of water and source of poison leaching into creeks and streams.

He wonders, *How can we change people's aesthetics? A bright green lawn is boring, not beautiful. Can they ever understand that a natural lawn filled with volunteer native plants is the most attractive and beneficial to bees, bunnies and birds? It can still be mowed and green and not need chemicals. Why do they insist on one species of grass and nothing else?*

Sometimes Gene uses the face mask his supervisor provides but it's usually too sticky hot and humid for that extra layer around his mouth and nose. Everyone assures everyone else these chemicals are safe, so why bother?

His 17-year-old daughter Tiffany graduates from high school today. Gene's wife will be furious if he misses the graduation ceremony which starts at 4:00. It's almost 2:30 and he's facing a 90-minute commute. He still has to return the day's unused chemicals to the warehouse which is required procedure, then shower and change.

I'm never gunna make it, Gene tells himself. There's no time to swing by the warehouse. Unfortunately, there's a larger load of unused product today. He's anxious, hungry, overheated and not thinking straight.

A new lawn went in at the house he's finishing up. The family hasn't moved in yet. He's alone with a big load of pesticide and decides to quietly get rid of it while no one is watching.

A narrow stream runs behind the house. Gene dumps the excess chemicals – about 26 gallons – into Mill Creek, a tributary of larger Nancy Creek. He has no idea Nancy Creek flows into the Chattahoochee River which runs for 100 miles through Atlanta and Georgia and dives into the Gulf of Mexico. His ignorant mistake will affect thousands of plants, fish, mammals, essential micro-organisms, amphibians, birds and people.

He jumps in his truck heading to Georgia 400, praying to get ahead of the gridlock.

*   *   *

Charlie's perspicacious hummingbird sees it all. She knows a disaster is about to hit.

She speeds over to Charlie's garden finding him pulling invasive Japanese Chaff Flower in his patch of woodland. Minutes before the bird arrives, Charlie's body fills with a nauseous gnawing. He's feeling the toxic poison slowly spreading and destroying everything it's touching but doesn't know the source.

That's when the hummingbird shows up to summon him. Her loud, low-pitched humming vibrates his inner ears. With such a quick metabolism, she looks frantic every day, but this is panic, darting and swooping furiously, gently pulling his uncombed hair. This is different.

"Problem. Big issue. Water. Issue. Poison. Water problem. Help us."

The anxious little hummer yanks Charlie's shirt collar now, insisting he follow her to the creek where he tends his mushrooms. She knows they have the power to stop the invisible poison floating toward the Chattahoochee River.

The creek is turning an opaque milky white, corroding everything as it flows.

"Problem. Big issue. Water. Issue. Poison. Problem. Help us."

It's faint, but Charlie smells a stench that's trouble. His brain is being overloaded, like a debilitating migraine pulsing with pain. He focuses every ounce of brain power with an intensity of intention he's never tapped before.

With penetrating concentration, Charlie urges all 45 species of fungi to expand and multiply in the moment, at hummingbird speed. With his mind, he activates the underground mycelium to swell together and form an intricately woven, solid sponge spreading across Nancy Creek like a bridge of veins and capillaries running and pumping fast.

Damage has already been done. A handful of tiny frogs and salamanders with bright blue tails are writhing helplessly as they float downstream, gasping their last breath. They won't make it.

Charlie's unique mushroom blend starts to unfold into a tough fungal fabric with tensile strength, interlocking fingers and laying down a solid wall of woven fibers that lock into both banks of the creek like a masterfully crafted beaver dam. Huge mushrooms rise out of the mycelium in weirdly shaped spheres and caps. Some have long waving fingers, some have giant chocolate brown gills, each one enhancing the wall's strength, getting stronger every second.

A pungent earthy aroma pours out of the mushroom dam as it soaks up the putrid chemical smell, sucking the poison, dissipating the potential for disaster. It's working.

Meltdown is averted by a wildly unlikely pair.

Charlie's healing powers leap to a new level of potency. He is exhausted and weak, feeling the physical toll such intense concentration requires. He's reeling with new knowledge and a powerful spirit of cross-species love and communication.

Silently, privately, Charlie and his tiny comrade save this tributary, preventing pure poison from spreading into the city and beyond.

*   *   *

That night, Charlie can't sleep. The day's crisis is a tipping point, upsetting to his core. Until now, he has suffered privately as he watches his neighborhood habitat being destroyed. He's remained a detached observer like a mature Tulip Poplar, taking it in silence. But he can't ignore it anymore. Something has to change.

As he taps into nature's diversity more deeply, he realizes he can no longer stand by passively. His powers are expanding to embrace nature's full force. It's time to tap into the venom
of the Copperhead and Rattlesnake,
aggressive tiger and territorial wolf,
violent ocean tsunami and turbulent volcano.
It's time to act.

"Show me exactly where the poison came from," he tells the hummer the next morning.

She too reaches a new level of desperation as she struggles to survive in this slice of the same migration route her ancestors have followed for 25 generations. This is her territory. She deserves to live here and thrive on her own terms.

Filled with renewed energy, she leads Charlie behind the new McMansion where Gene made the illegal dump. The exact point of entry is obvious.

Grasses and vines in that swath have already shriveled up, lifeless and crispy brown.

That's when Gene's truck barrels up the steep driveway. Charlie gathers the courage to confront him.

"I know what you did."

"Whut are you talkin' about, kid?"

"I know you dumped a big load of chemicals into the creek right here. How could you be so careless? That stuff will kill thousands of living things and pollute the water for miles downstream."

"You don't know nuthin' about it, kid. I use this stuff like it says in the directions. It's harmless. It's legal. And my clients pay good money for it. Now git lost."

"But it's not harmless," Charlie insists. "It's poison. You overloaded the creek with it and those chemicals will linger for years."

Gene notices Charlie's eyes – one pale sky blue, the other emerald moss green.

"What kind a hippie freak are you? You don't know whut yur talkin' about. This is private property and you're trespassin'. I have a job to git done." Gene raises his voice to yelling. "Git lost. Now."

Charlie backs away, walking backward down the sloping driveway staring right through Gene Jenkins' ignorance. *If you won't believe my words, I'll make it clear another way*, Charlie thinks to himself. He starts orchestrating a plan.

* * *

When Gene returns to the property two weeks later, he's in for a surprise. He begins re-spraying where a few tiny weeds sprout. Two squirrels appear on the front lawn and boldly get closer. "Get outta here," Gene says, shaking his poison wand in their direction. Amazingly, they don't run off. They move closer and both stand up on two hind legs.

Four chunky fat beavers stumble out of the Wax Myrtle shrubs near the creek and stand on hind legs too, staring at Gene. Their puffy faces grimace, flashing square buck teeth, stained orangey brown from chewing pine resin.

Then six raccoons slink up the slope – faces jutting out first, masked like bandits. Their long legs are like beatnik jazz dancers from the '50s in black tights and heels with ringed tail pizzazz. Three are hissing; two are clucking loudly, clearly irritated.

All three lines rise up on two hind legs. The entire chorus groans louder with mean hissing and spitting in Gene's direction, ready to attack.

"What the hell's goin' on here?" Gene says out loud. He can't get them to run away. The aggressive animals hold their ground, showing sharp teeth in every size, ready to bite.

Gene is forced to leave, totally confused. He tries to finish up the small lawn in back when a stunning Ruby-Throated Hummingbird dives so near his head that he hears the purring hum rattle his eardrum.

Boy, that was close. How weird, he is thinking. As he sprays, the iridescent bird plunges right into the toxic mist and instantly drops dead to the ground.

Gene is completely baffled. *What the hell?* He's too freaked out to go near the dead bird, leaving her right where she fell. Yes, it's Charlie's cherished friend. Her patience ran out. Compelled to sacrifice herself as a bold attempt to get through to the lame ones.

Visibly shaken, Gene gets in his truck and calls it a day. Stuck in Georgia 400 traffic, he tries to make sense of the crazy encounters. But he can't. An hour later, as he enters his wooded neighborhood, he buzzes down the windows to let the cool evening oxygen in.

Within seconds, two bats swoop in targeting his head, fluttering between the back of his skull and the truck's headrest. *Jesus. That's the biggest damn moth I ever saw,* he tells himself, trying to swat it behind his head. He has to pull over and jump out of the truck. That's when he discovers it's two reddish gray bats with oversized, watery black eyes staring him down, barring their teeth and hissing. "This is fucking frightening," he mutters.

It takes about 10 minutes to finally get the bats to leave his front seat. He arrives home pale and shaking. "What happened to you, Gene?" his wife Judy asks. "You look terrible. What's the matter?"

"You won't believe it," Gene says. "It's nothin'. I don't wanna talk about it."

He sits in silence the rest of the evening, pondering the squirrels, beavers, raccoons, the hummingbird, bats. *What is the damn connection? Am I hallucinating or getting dementia?*

Gene goes to bed early, completely exhausted. While he's asleep, a rainstorm rolls through. It's a strong one with loud thunder and vicious winds. A tall Loblolly Pine in his driveway is struck by a lightning bolt and the whole thing is uprooted, smacking right down the middle of his truck, totaling it.

When Gene wakes up to the destruction, he's speechless. He feels his life crashing in on him, knowing something is terribly wrong. He can barely rally enough energy to call his supervisor to say he's too sick to come in today. He sinks into a deep depression as his world unravels. He's now convinced those weird encounters are signs he can't go back to his job at ChemLawn. He's done. *Maybe that stuff really is poison.*

Gene doesn't know it yet, but by the end of the year he'll be diagnosed with Stage 3 colon cancer.

*   *   *

Before his heroic hummingbird goes suicidal, she telegraphs Charlie a goodbye plea. Charlie follows the radar vibrations and finds her stiff little body. Heartbroken, he carries her home to his garden and lovingly digs a grave under the *Salvia guaranitica* she was so fond of with its deep blue flowers perfectly designed for her sleek long beak.

Salvia guaranitica

He also adds Oyster mushrooms to neutralize the toxic chemicals in her beautiful body, and save the *Salvia.*

Boy: *Losing you was never part of the plan.*

Bird: *I was ready to go.*
Remember me, Charlie.
Cherish me.
We loved across two species.
We're on the same team.
Even now.

Chapter 9 – Grandpa's Journals

This morning, Charlie's dead mom shows up in a vivid dream. He can't shake the image and the knot in his gut.

Jill lies nude on the forest floor looking up at crowns of the tallest poplars and pines, smiling as if floating in a luxurious bubble bath. Two large, blonde snakes are shedding their skins nearby, slimy and moist.

She sees Charlie staring in wonder and signals him to come closer. He lies down beside her as a huge owl swoops into the scene wearing an emerald-green velvet cape that's also a long tail touching the ground, creating a gentle breeze as the giant bird passes silently overhead.

Hundreds of Monarch butterflies emerge from behind an ancient Beech. They land on its limbs to soak up the sun then stack their fragile bodies on top of each other like Pringles fitting together, forming two dense piles. It's all jaw-droppingly beautiful, humid and lush.

The fantasy is pierced when the alarm goes off.

He's always looking for clues to understand his mom, curious about how she came to love and worship nature. The dream hurts his heart, still in anguish because they never had the chance to know and love each other.

* * *

No one ever goes into the attic, but Hank's client asked for original negatives from many years ago. Hank thinks they might be up there. While he's rummaging around dusty castoffs, Hank spots a large box in the corner where some of Jill's favorite clothes are still packed away. The words DAD'S JOURNALS are written in Jill's bold handwriting with a purple magic marker. He's never seen this box before.

Hank waits to open it until Charlie gets home from his job in the biology lab at Georgia Tech. After dinner, Hank tells his son he found a surprise, and he wants Charlie to be the first to take a peek. Stacked inside are about 20 classic black and white composition journals spanning the late '60s to the late '80s created by Jill's artistic dad, Ernest.

They appear to be right off the desk of Russell Crowe in the film *A Beautiful Mind*. Each page is jam-packed with strange collages and hand-drawn charts of numbers and symbols as if he's counting or tracking messages from beyond the Milky Way.

The pages are also filled with black and white photos, precisely trimmed from newspapers, an old medium that went extinct in 2022. Faces of Ronald Reagan, Marilyn Monroe, FDR, Andy Warhol and Abraham Lincoln appear over and over. Most pages also have frames of black and white newspaper comic strips, adding levity and bold visuals. Brenda Starr is a favorite. Charlie thought comic strips only came in full color.

"These are incredible," Charlie says in awe. While Jill's journals are filled edge to edge with only words, her dad's books are predominantly visual with thick textures of layered paper. Every page is yellow-brown along the edges from age.

"I've been given a whole new treasure chest of clues and messages about who Mom's father is and who she comes from," Charlie tells his dad. "I can't wait to share these weird works of art with Ella."

*   *   *

After a few weeks of studying the new material, it starts to make sense. Ernest is tracking various stocks, day by day, in three portfolios – an

IRA, a personal account and one for his business. On a page dated 3/7/86, the total is at $4,776,699.

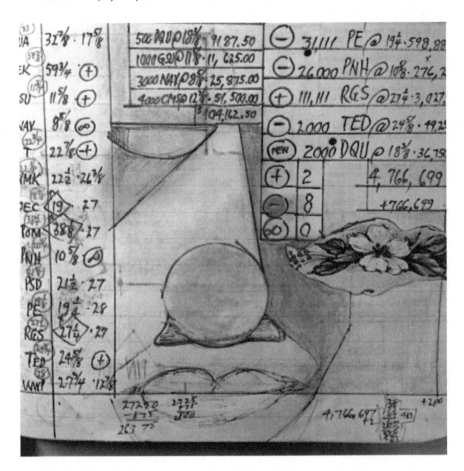

Charlie will never know these journals are highly influenced by his grandfather smoking pot all day as a portal to his creativity – masking and self-medicating his emotional pain in a private world of self-imposed isolation. Flinging himself into a constant dream state, Ernest creates his own visual language with scissors, black Pentel felt tip pens and Pritt glue sticks.

He's killing time as he waits for hourly stock reports on radios in every room, mapping his own inner journey while tracking his fortune. The marijuana buzz gives him the laser focus to cut and paste and play like he's a young kid again.

Lines of poetry scatter throughout the pages, revealing new and strange puzzle pieces for Charlie to ponder and dissect. Ernest was obviously a keen observer of nature too.

1/72
We shall walk down a stream, long for a mountain, eat a plate of possibilities.

A blue jay makes a perfect landing on the branch of a pink dogwood.

The soft inquisitive breeze is constant as change, powerful as wind.

A traffic jam of thoughts in the mad house of your memory.
Now I'm smoking the dust of many roads.

And this line matches an idea Charlie remembers from Jill's pages one winter.

Ernest: Naked trees that are skeletons of themselves become modest.

Jill: On the bleakest winter day, trees stand black naked above thick blankets of snow below. Their colorful leaves are a distant memory, reduced to twisted wet trunks with frozen fingers grasping for clouds.

One of the books is filled with Ernest's poems, no visuals.

A SCOTCH
ON 57th STREET

CHAMPAGNE
AT THE DRAKE.

You PAY THE BARTENDER
WITH
MOSS MORE PRECIOUS
THAN
EMERALDS

FOR YOU KNOW-

SOMEWHERE
ON A
DISTANT HILL
THERE IS

BLOOD AND FUR
IN A
NEST 1/72

Charlie marvels how not one collaged piece pulls away from the page even after so many years. Did his grandfather intentionally put the extra time in to make sure these books would last well beyond his lifetime? He must have known these pages would be discovered and revered in the future.

He has plenty of time on his hands because of the agoraphobic loner he becomes. The intricate pages are his lifeline.

Decades later, every page slightly sticks to the next because they've been pressed together so tightly, unexposed to air and daylight until now. What if these books were never found? They could have been doomed to obscurity if Charlie didn't see their value and absorb the lessons they hold.

* * *

He's falling in love with his grandfather Ernest, a relative he will never meet.

Ernest and his Jaguar XKE

Ernest's private office is on the third floor of his 1920s mansion in Rochester, New York where he hides like a bad boy being punished. Punishing himself.

In another era, the cramped space served as servants' quarters with three small bedrooms and a shared bathroom. He calls it the Third World. His own staff is never allowed up those stairs. It's his secret hiding place to smoke and daydream, track his fortune and make his art.

When Jill and her sister Julie are in their 20s, they're given access to his private universe where he indoctrinates them with his bizarre philosophies and craziness. *Never get married. It's an outdated institution.*

He sees himself as a wise man, the ultimate hero. The pot — and having plenty of money — exaggerates his narcissistic confidence to live the dream, encouraged by capturing faces of contemporary idols he snips and collects in his journals. FDR, Abraham Lincoln, Frank Sinatra, George Washington and Ronald Reagan are slices of his dream persona, feeding delusions of power in his own twisted mind.

The amount of time and tedious hand work involved is remarkable, like a fine quilter or haute couture seamstress. It's astonishing how the artist follows such strict rituals of his own making.

Ernest is also teaching himself new vocabulary words scattered on the edges, sometimes with definitions. Words like ennui, polemic, sententious and misogamist, "one who hates marriage."

* * *

Charlie makes another thrilling connection.

Self-portraits in the journals are sketches of Ernest's face that eventually become the two-foot-tall bronze mask that still leans against an Ash tree in Jill's back garden. Charlie never knew its origin. Imagine the egotistical drive it takes to commission a larger-than-life solid bronze effigy of your own face and head.

Bronze head, two feet tall

Ernest frequently draws the mask as if captivated with his own myth, intrigued with his own face. Way before Facebook and selfies.

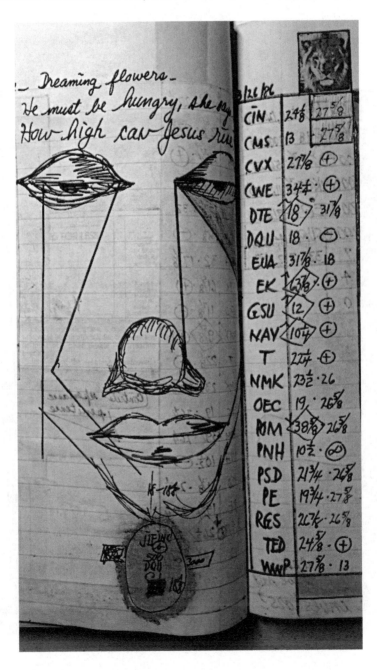

Several journal pages feature Xerox copies of the bronze head before it's painted in bold African colors.

Chapter 10 – Ella's Love Journals

Ella selfie with Hellebores

Inspired by reading Jill's journals, Ella starts her own. These random ex-cerpts reveal her sweet love for Charlie, feeling sure they're meant to be together and yet full of doubt.

March 15, 2029

When you were inside me by the lake
the birds stopped singing as if holding their breath
taking in the moment right with us.
Did you notice?
In the silence, we had another chance to start the world again.
As if we were the only ones on Earth, reinventing civilization.

When the rains stopped, the bird songs came back at full volume.
A mama bluebird and her babies swoop in as if they wanted to be closer to you.

You inspire me to be the real me
You inspire me to be more of ME
to care about every blade of grass, feather and spider web as you do.

Organic orgasmic.
Far from mechanic.
Authentic and expansive – cracking me wide open like an ostrich egg.
Your touch unlocks my fears, helping me let them go.
When he finally calls on Friday, I say, "Is this the gorgeous animal I encoun-
tered in the woods last weekend?" He just laughs.

November 2, 2030
When I hesitated to leap to the next rock, you told me "Believe in yourself."
I let go of my fear and it worked. I want to believe in myself. I want to be-
lieve in us.
Feels like we still have so many adventures to experience together.
I love how you pick up on nature's tiny details.
Most guys are addicted to their phones and sports and don't get it.

August 20, 2031
I love the idea of using nature in fashion. Not illustrations of flowers but
actual photos of Charlie's rare flowers blown up huge on tight-fitting T-
shirts.

If men and women wore nature on their chests, vests, sleeves, dresses and
skirts, wouldn't they care about it more?
Speak up to save it?

Would he be a biz partner with me?
Would he be a life partner with me?
Or are we too young to make that huge decision now? Why not? How
could I do better? Who could be more beautiful inside and out?

Or is he from another planet?

Your skin is silky soft like royalty.
You are a royal prince from a distant star.

Refined diamond in the rough.
Do I deserve a prince? Yes! I am a princess with Polish roots.
I'm learning to appreciate your special qualities that no one else has.

Is this a real word? – Ecologic.
What does it mean?
Is it a way to teach kids about nature?
What would our kid be like if Charlie and I ever got pregnant?
Super sensitive, super smart, super talented.

It's Charlie's birthday this week and I'm working on a handmade card with dried ferns and seeds.

You are exquisite on so many levels.
I'm on your team all the way.
I want to be in your life.
Now and in the future.
Love always,
Ella

Is that too strong? He prefers to communicate not in words but with his gorgeous two-toned eyes, his mind and his gentle curious fingers.
I think I'm falling too fast, too much.
I'm afraid to ask what he wants from me if anything.

September 12, 2031
It feels like I've known you for thousands of years. A timeless connection. I feel close to you and distant too. When you get that far-away daydream gaze, feels like I've lost you. What would it be like if we lived together? I would love sleeping next to you every night. Would I ever stop feeling the thrill of being next to you, thigh to thigh? Would it finally wear off? I can't believe the chemistry we have will fade. It's too charged. It's too good a fit.

Can our love ever be as strong and long-lasting as these fantasy couples in old movies I love like Dances with Wolves and The American President?

John and Yoko were the real deal. Are we?

Maybe we can make great art together or save the planet one day.
Let's try.
Please try with me.

October 7, 2031
When I was a kid, my parents didn't allow comic books or Dr. Suess, since the author was a John Bircher. Instead, I had art books with the vibrant fantasy world of Marc Chagall. The rich colors and kinetic shapes of Kandinsky. The smiling faces of Paul Klee. And the far-out imagination of Picasso showing me there are endless ways to see a chair, a face or a still life.

Looking back, I now appreciate how they were exposing me to a deeper visual language.

By seeing the world through the eyes of great artists, my young mind opened to new perspectives at an early age. I learned to recognize real art and see beyond the childish fluff most people love as popular culture.

Is this why I can appreciate Charlie's way of seeing?

Chapter 11 – Aunt Julie's Letter

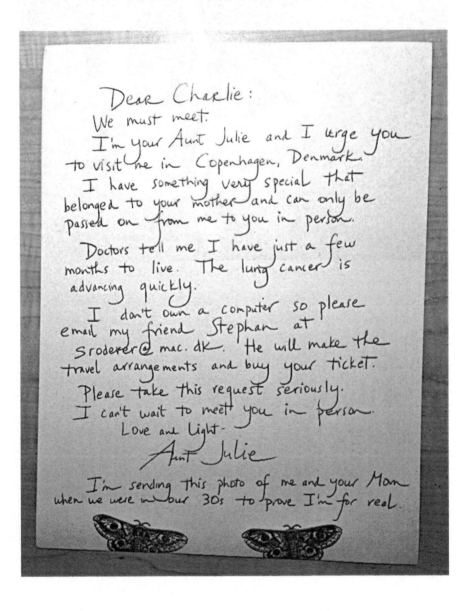

Dear Charlie:

We must meet.

I'm your Aunt Julie and I urge you to visit me in Copenhagen, Denmark.

I have something very special that belonged to your mother and can only be passed on from me to you in person.

Doctors tell me I have just a few months to live. The lung cancer is advancing quickly.

I don't own a computer so please email my friend Stephan at Sroderer@mac.dk. He will make the travel arrangements and buy your ticket.

Please take this request seriously. I can't wait to meet you in person.

Love and Light-

Aunt Julie

I'm sending this photo of me and your Mom when we were in our 30s to prove I'm for real.

Sisters Julie and Jill, Earth Day in Atlanta, 2000

Chapter 12 – Earthbound

Julie's letter upsets him. Charlie heard his mother has a sister, but he knows nothing about her. And it's the thought of flying that throws him off.

Charlie's mind is full of doubt and resistance. He tells himself, *People aren't designed to fly in metal tubes. We're meant to walk the Earth on our own two feet. Slowly with eyes, ears and nose wide open. Seeing. Touching. Listening. Smelling. Sensing.*

It feels so wrong to be looking down higher than any mountain, missing the details. I don't even like riding in cars. I feel trapped inside a metal box on wheels going way too fast.

It's called amaxophobia – fear of riding in a vehicle.

He knows aviation is a polluting, high-impact industry. That's another reason he's never flown before.

Jet fuel pours into the skies every day, poisoning the outer atmosphere. Accumulating there. No one even talks about that. Until Greta Thunberg.

I don't want to be part of it. I live my life differently on purpose. I'm more comfortable right here, rooted in rich soil like my mushrooms and trees where there's still plenty to discover.

But I say I want to know my mother. Julie must be the closest person to Jill on the planet. What can I learn from her? Who is my real family anyway? Hank and Jill? Or maple, fox and river?

Am I limited to human time? Or connected to timeless seeds and stars? I have memories from before I was born, stretching back hundreds, maybe thousands of years. I hear voices and songs others don't hear.

I'm more connected to the Cherokee who lived on this land first. And yet I go back even further, remembering dinosaurs, watching them trample original dense forests. Feeling related to those gigantic, beautiful creatures too.

The Cherokee were so fascinating and smart. They could read the rivers, interpret the stars, understand bird songs, decipher and predict the weather and planets rising. They could identify animal tracks, translate the calls of wolves and owls, use every single plant as healing medicine. They made decisions based on how nature works. Their priority was to understand her, not abuse her.

Today, everything is focused on high tech. Faster jets. Faster computers. Simple, instant answers. That's the opposite of nature's design.

What if history was flipped? What if Cherokee chiefs won the wars against invaders from England and Spain? What if that wisdom survived and today's leaders were authentic native people? We would be wiser. Caring for the Earth would be top priority.
If only we could shift the focus from money and technology and put nature first. Why is that so hard to grasp? If only our culture would put a high value on forests, clean air and water, and live in tune with nature the way our ancestors did.

The planet would be such a different place. Civilization could be flourishing. In balance. Instead, it's on a crash course to self-destruct. Why did we throw away those valuable survival skills passed down over generations?

That night Charlie dreams his body rising into the sky beyond his control. His bones turn to smoke, fragile, transparent, still rising. He's lost his soul, reduced to nothingness – still rising higher into the clouds, feeling helpless and sad since he is no longer himself.

Days later, Charlie rakes leaves on his small patch of lawn, spreading them under the shrubs as nutritious mulch. Orange and yellow leaves are still falling from maples nearby. They twist and glide as if enjoying one last freefall release before they hit the ground forever and begin to break down, returning to soil. He wants to play with that downward motion. Raising his arms like a symphony conductor, Charlie directs the leaves to float upward again.

They follow his movements, getting a second chance to spin and dance in the wind. Each leaf has its own quiet little voice saying, *"Wheeee heeee. One more roller coaster ride."* Charlie controls their falls, conducting the chorus. It makes him laugh out loud.

Ella is knocking at the front door. When she doesn't get an answer, she walks around to the backyard and stumbles upon this mind-blowing scene. She stops in time to hide behind a wide pine trunk to keep observing without Charlie knowing. Another gust of wind shakes even more leaves from wooden outstretched arms. As they continue to fall, Charlie's graceful gestures guide them right back up to glide and soar, then down, then back up, directing their movement to twirl in tight circles several times before he lets them land.

He hears a favorite sound – the loud shrill of the Pileated woodpecker (*Dryocopus pileatus*). Its piercing voice resonates from the treetops sounding like the wild laugh of an old woman going insane. Standing almost two feet tall, these powerful birds with genetic links to dinosaurs take full advantage of the dead trees Charlie leaves on his property where the woodpeckers can pound away for tasty insects. The gorgeous redheaded bird drops down closer to deliver a message.

Then it lands right on Charlie's head, balancing itself perfectly! Charlie is startled yet flattered the woodpecker wants to be so close. Its strong talons lift up and down as if walking in place, enjoying the feel of Charlie's soft hair. Ella's jaw drops open as she imagines a living headdress or enormous crown on the head of a Native American prince. Both ornament and human are in sync. While still balancing on top of his head, the magnificent bird bends down to whisper in Charlie's ear. *"Alert. Alert. Be ready to receive an alert from our ancestors. Flying is part of living. Be on alert."*

With its message transmitted, the bird flies straight up, disappearing into the thickest part of the canopy.

Ella's blood is racing. She's almost dizzy after witnessing this incredible encounter. She takes a few breaths and Charlie turns toward her, always glad to see her.

"That bird was communicating with you," Ella says in amazement.

"He was. It was so cool to have him touching me. He said be open to another bigger message coming my way," Charlie explains. An odd sensation rushes through him, as if feathers are fluttering all over his back and arms.

"You really must be from another planet," Ella smiles as she gives him a tight hug which helps ground her.

Intimate contact with the woodpecker keeps Charlie especially happy for several days. At the same time, he's suffering from inner turmoil, pressured to decide about Copenhagen. He writes to Julie's friend and reluctantly agrees to make the trip. Soon after, the ticket is booked so he's forced to go, already dreading it.

*　　*　　*

Atlanta's airport is the most active in the world. It couldn't be in more stark contrast to the natural places Charlie feels comfortable.

As he exits the MARTA train, he's swept into the crowds rushing and crushing around him. He immediately starts going into meltdown. Too many people. Lighting harsh. Sounds jarring. His eyes start burning as he picks up chemical smells of cleaning solvent and plastic packaging emanating from every corner. The scene is devoid of nature, mechanized and sterile. He's getting sick already.

Long security lines of people treated like cattle to slaughter. This is worse than any nightmare he could dream up – a painful collision of his careful, slower pace with their hectic, computerized world. He watches as security guards with guns on their hips and dangling shiny handcuffs make each passenger raise arms above their head, opening their hearts to radiation in plastic tubes. People are taking off belts and shoes as they empty their pockets.

As his turn approaches, he gives up too easily. *This is too much. Let me out of here.*

The only way out is zigzagging back through the long security line against the grain, brushing people as he passes. They stare with irritated, scowling faces. He's determined to escape.

A wild animal caged.

Charlie remembers reading about a new park built by the Flint Riverkeeper as they begin to reclaim natural tributaries that still remain. The headwaters of this mighty river were literally paved over to build the Atlanta airport. The Flint survived anyway, flowing more than 300 miles south of the airport to the Gulf Coast, making it one of the few rivers in the country that travel such a distance.

Walking quickly, fueled by heavy breathing, Charlie spots an open field and pocket of straggly trees. He's drawn to it and stumbles upon a skinny, forgotten tributary. Throwing his backpack to the ground, he lays face up, spine connecting to Earth, plugging back into an essential life force. He's melting into the grass, feeling healing sun rays on his face, sensing magnetic energy from Earth's core. He tries to channel that energy into his limbs to recharge and re-center his equilibrium, beginning to detox from the severe culture clash.

His breathing finally starts to calm. Fond memories of a canoe trip on the Flint with Hank, Phillip and two of Hank's college friends are washing over him. Charlie was just six years old – mesmerized by the timeless beauty of old-growth cedars reaching straight out of the water, and how utterly quiet it was. Only the sound of paddles piercing the smooth green surface. Completely engulfed in nature. Not a man-made structure in sight.

His daydream is interrupted by the high-volume roar of a jet coming in close for a landing.

Man, am I glad I'm not on one of those, he tells himself. He's still too sensitive and ill-equipped to be trapped inside a giant machine, so far from his sacred ground at home.

As the warm afternoon light dissipates toward dusk, he's finally grounded enough to make a move. Charlie returns to the MARTA train. All he wants to do is head home to the Lenox station.

Feeling defeated, he promptly emails Stephan in Denmark saying not to expect him. All he can do is be honest. He apologizes for the hassle, saying he got overwhelmed in the airport and isn't ready for the long flight.

Sure, he feels embarrassed when he has to tell the story to his dad and Ella. Maybe in time, he can try again. Just not now.

"You're overthinking this, Charlie. You can do it," Ella tells him. "We can't stop those jets. They're going to fly there anyway so you might as well take one of the seats. It would be fantastic to go to a European city and explore a new culture. Especially with you."

"You mean you would come with me? If you were there, maybe I could do it."

"Of course, I'll go with you. I would love to."

And then she kisses him.

*   *   *

Sandhill crane in flight

Sandhill cranes (*Grus canadensis*) have migrated along the same routes for tens of thousands of years. A large population of almost 70,000 birds, summers in Nebraska and Canada. One of their resting spots is along the Hiawasee River near Cleveland, Tennessee. From there, they fly directly over Atlanta to winter in south Georgia and Florida.

Bones of these magnificent creatures, who stand four feet tall, are found in fossils dating back three million years or more. Even with countless manmade intrusions on their habitat, they still survive here unchanged. They're slow to reproduce like the cedar trees that root nearby along the Hiawasee; both species almost went extinct. Cranes learn from their parents how and where to migrate. Like tiny hummingbirds.

Imagine how their flight path over Atlanta has changed from a heavily forested dense green carpet to the mega-city it's become – paved over, degraded, polluted and electrified.

Traveling in chevron formation in groups of 50 to several hundred, they fly higher than any other bird. Yet their constant honking is so loud it can be heard from the ground. Atlanta is just a place to pass through, ironically, like millions of people do each year, changing planes at Atlanta's Harts-field-Jackson International Airport.

As Charlie walks around his garden, still trying to regain composure and a sense of peace, he hears a flock of about 200 cranes honking overhead. The elongated V patterns are a soothing sight accompanied by their strange, vivid music. The sandhills fly high above his garden every November so he's been expecting these flocks to pass overhead and keep moving. But something remarkable happens. Two of the giant birds break away and descend to Earth, heading right for Charlie. The elegant, steel-grey birds are seeking him out.

As they approach, their long skinny legs splay out for a landing. Charlie freezes so he won't startle them, though he's in shock. They never stop in Atlanta.

Sandhill cranes mate for life so this must be a married pair. The scarlet red skin patches on top of their bald heads are luminous. Needlepoint beaks raise skyward, flexing elegant, elongated necks. Charlie bows his head slightly and looks right into their round, orange eyes, backlit like glowing jack-o-lanterns. Their complex eyes see in every direction with superior abilities to scan the full view from high altitudes, seeing more than any human ever can.
Charlie trembles inside, knowing how rare this is. He deliberately keeps still to make the birds feel comfortable and welcome.

When resting on the ground, the honking changes to a constant cooing and gentle gurgling deep in their long, tall throats – a beautifully haunting melody that never ends. One bird steps closer, whispering that distinctive music. As Charlie listens closely, the gurgles start to make sense. She has something she wants to say.

"Don't give in to fear, Magic Boy.
Believe us, we know how wrong and destructive jet planes are.
Their increase is obscene, but we deal with it.

*They clog our sacred migration paths that were once wide open and clear
for only us.*
Now jets and small planes are constantly in our way.

*But we can't turn back time. This is what humans do to upset the natural
balance.*
There's no doubt they are the most destructive species that ever lived.
They force every other creature to adjust to their ways or perish.
We know you're different.
*You're caught in the middle since you're born human but with added vision
and sensibilities.*
Yin, yang, my man.

Don't fight the insanity.
You have to rise above it as we do.
You will make it safely to Europe.
You are needed there to meet with your clan.
Go."

The giant birds stretch and sway their necks in graceful curves, waiting for
his answer. How can Charlie resist? He nods and accepts the challenge.

"I understand," he assures them. "I can't just live in one protected place
and never leave. If you can fly thousands of miles on giant wings, I can sit
inside a jet and visit faraway places too. Thank you for encouraging me
and for helping me understand your exquisite language."

"You will go far, Magic Boy. With great vision comes responsibility.
Manmade ideas and machines are meaningless clutter.
Riding in their jet is the easy part."

Sounds of muffled honking come closer from high above. It's time to join
the next flock of 400 birds, continuing south to Georgia's Okefenokee
Swamp. The visitors' tremendous wings start flapping, generating a soothing breeze. Their necks stretch straight out as far as they can go, lifting off
above Charlie's head into the sun.

With Ella's willingness to join him and now this magnificent encounter, there's no question. Charlie believes he can do this.

*   *   *

The next morning, a second letter from Aunt Julie arrives.

Dear Charlie,
Stephan told me you're hesitant to come here.
You've never traveled before. I understand.
Trust me. You will love it here.
And we have important family business.

I regret we've never met. That's my fault.
My life is almost over, so now is the time.

Money is not an issue.
Please, please say yes.

Love to you and see you soon,
Aunt Julie

Chapter 13 – Sexual Healing

*Diamorpha grows in shallow solution pits
on granite outcrops like Arabia Mountain*

One of Charlie's favorite plants, the endangered *Diamorpha,* only blooms on Arabia Mountain in March. He invites Ella to join him for a picnic on Sunday since she's never seen the lacy white blossoms on vivid red stems.

Spending time on a 400-million-year-old hunk of granite feels like walking on another planet. Timeless and rock solid. Jill was friendly with the planners of Arabia Mountain Park who wisely determined to keep it wild, unlike its younger sister – commercialized Stone Mountain.

Charlie knows a secret pine grove near Alexander Lake where no one will find them. It's a glorious spring day and the temperature should hit 80 degrees soon after they arrive.

Because of recent rains, Charlie brings a plastic tablecloth as a moisture barrier then stretches out a soft fleecy blanket on top. He has a plan.

"Lie down with me before we eat," Charlie says. The young couple gets comfortable soaking up the sun. Ella's head rests on his tall chest. She follows his heartbeat. Safe and calm.

Charlie wants to be nude like two wild animals. He lifts Ella's turquoise T-shirt over her head to remove it.

"Really? Are you sure no one will see us?"

"I'm sure. I've been here many times. Trust me."

She does trust him as she lets him take her shirt off, then the pencil gray camisole she wears instead of a bra. Scanning the scene in every direction, now she looks straight into his blue and green eyes as she unzips her jeans and lies next to him naked. Charlie slips his clothes off too.

They've always loved the simple act of holding hands. Every time, Ella cherishes how much warmth radiates from his palms, comforting and supporting her.

"How many different ways can we hold hands?" Ella asks. "I bet there's an infinite number of positions just for our hands." She moves his hands to touch hers, palm to palm. Pressing harder for even more heat. Then the back of his hand to her palm. Wrapping curved fingers. Straightening fingers. Interweaving fingers. Holding on tight.

He exhales deeply, attempting to leave the present behind, reaching backward in time. With eyes closed, his mind searches for signs when Native Americans used this mountain for sacred rituals. He's certain they made love here too. He dreams back even further to when dinosaurs climbed this mountain. He imagines Ella and himself as the only humans.

Ella's never done it outside before. She's scared and at the same time aroused, trying to let herself flow with his wishes. She knows Charlie is cautious and thoughtful and wouldn't put her in danger. So, she climbs on top as he pulls her even closer, his long slender fingers wrapping tightly around her petite waist. Their special blend of magnetic chemistry pulses through them. It's too powerful to stop. No reason to stop.

Out of nowhere, dark gray clouds move in and a gentle rain begins to fall. Muted thunder moans in the distance.

"Oh, no. We'll get soaked," she says.

"It's okay. It feels good," Charlie assures her. "It's warm. It's sensual. Just feel it, Ella."

Now she's wet inside and out. Charlie is deep inside her imagining he's a huge cat – a California mountain lion or a Florida panther, licking and drinking the raindrops rolling between her breasts. Drinking Ella in.

Suddenly it's pouring. Her instinct is to separate from him and cover up. He won't let her go. For him the drenching rain is erotic, encouraging him to keep their bodies fused, melting into each other even further. She is swimming in new territory, abandoning her doubts.

His tongue feels so warm and strong on her soaked breast, then utterly gentle on her nipple. She's a mermaid princess riding a muscular dolphin.

He's feline; she's the ocean. Every touch bridges the distance between their worlds. Grasping to close the gap between every man and woman, between species.

Unable to hold off any longer, Ella ripples to a climax at the exact moment a silver lightning bolt shoots straight down to the horizon. BOOM. Thunder crackles directly overhead. *Is he orchestrating the sky to respond to our bodies?* she wonders. Swept up in the dreamy magic of it all, she's convinced no one else could ever give her this much pleasure. She's transported to another galaxy, soaring way above the limits of her body.

Charlie beams back at her with a radiant smile showing he approves of her being adventurous and believing in him.

While trees appear to move excruciatingly slow by human measure, one process does move swiftly. During heavy storms like this, water flows at about 20 inches a minute from subterranean tree roots in thin passages moving straight up to leaves and canopy. Charlie feels the parallel as his own blood rises, flowing straight upward. He can hear rushing sounds from delicate streams of rainwater racing up through the pine trunks, quenching and nurturing his brother trees.

Now gasping for air, Ella reluctantly brings her awareness back to Earth. The rain moves out as suddenly as it rushed in. Golden sunshine breaks through again, warming their moist juicy skin.

Birds fly in overhead, singing at full volume. Charlie recognizes the song. It's a rare family of Bluebirds. Ella's sure they're drawn to Charlie's presence. A mother and two babies land on a pine branch near the lovers' heads. They watch the baby birds test and stretch their wings, still too timid to fly yet.

Charlie feels they're mocking him and his own fear of flying. As the mother bird encourages her chicks, she's also encouraging him to take flight.
Fly to Denmark to meet Aunt Julie.
Go for lift-off to love Ella as your lifelong partner.

They stare into each other's eyes again, penetrating below the surface. Charlie rolls on top, pressing his full weight into her bones. Ella bursts out laughing, even though he's heavy. His imagination zooms inside the marrow of her skeleton. Now his thoughts probe the warm, soft spaces between every vertebra – tapping into her life force.

Subconsciously without knowing, she senses he's reaching into her ligaments, capillaries and muscles never explored before. She wraps her long legs around him, pulling him closer. She wants their bodies to melt into a singular being and create an entirely new person from their love and trust. Her thoughts wander to his childhood, remembering he never knew his mother's love. *Is that why he's guarded and distant with most people? Can I break through to him? We're breaking into new layers of love right now.*

Charlie feels it too. He's never been this comfortable with anyone. He knows he's strange. *Can she accept how different I am? It feels like she can.*

He's never had a real friend before. Her sensibilities are in tune with his. *Ella, I want you near me always.*

She lovingly nibbles his ears, his cheeks. She's hoping he hears her heart reaching out, urging him to always stay close. With her kisses, she wants to show him how they can grow together over a lifetime, choosing an uncharted path carved precisely for them.

They start kissing long and hard. Then deeper. Then deeper. Touching the tips of their tongues, moving them around each other's lips and teeth. Reaching for true connection.

Finally, Charlie comes up for air. "I'm sensing mushrooms nearby."

Within seconds, a patch of silver Oyster mushrooms breaks through the mulch of rotting leaves on fallen oak branches – unfurling in fast motion. Then more and more pop up around their blanket, multiplying like speeding clouds. Charlie's brain waves are coaxing them out.

"I'm not even surprised anymore," Ella tells him. "You have an incredible gift. You really are a superpower."

"The fantastic part is I'm not doing it alone. I'm channeling the energies between *us* – you and me together. Our forces combined are stronger than mine alone."

That's when Ella realizes she can have a role in his world. Their bond is more solid at this moment than ever. Solid as the granite stretching out around them in every direction. She fills his doubts with love. He completes her unrealized hopes.

"I'm starving," Ella smiles. "What did you bring?"

Charlie produces two perfectly ripe avocados, her favorite fruit. Slicing one in half, he hands her a spoon. He even remembers a squeeze of lime. "Yum. How perfect. Thank you, Charlie. You really know me."

He pulls a handmade ceramic plate from his pack and arranges smoked salmon on crispy flat bread. She adds purple grapes and orange slices. They devour it.

Before they go, Charlie uses his pen knife to slice fresh mushrooms at the base. "How about these for a delicious dinner?"

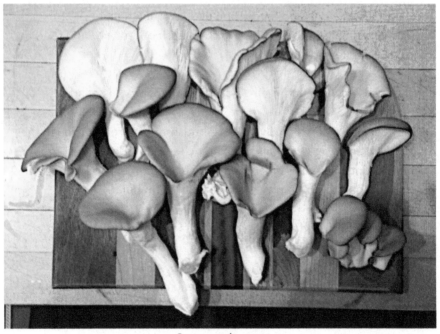

Oyster mushrooms

Chapter 14 – Copenhagen Transfer

Charlie and Ella land at Copenhagen's Kastrup Airport ready for adventure. The flight was easy, bolstered by Ella's loving presence.

Freetown Christiania is their destination, the counterculture haven where Aunt Julie lives.

Back in 1971, a bold tribe of hippies took over an abandoned military complex from the early 1600s. The urban island spans 84 acres.

These cultural pioneers were determined to give birth to an autonomous, egalitarian and peaceful society, writing their own rules, governing themselves by consensus. The city of Copenhagen was cool with it since no one else wanted the dilapidated site back then. Today the real estate is desirable and hip.

Two generations of anarchists, artists and freethinkers flourish here on their own terms. Julie fits right in as someone who always steered clear of convention.

Christiania mural with goddesses and mushrooms

Walls are covered with colorful graffiti. There's lots of vegan cafés, bookstores and bike shops. Lush gardens overflow their boundaries. Established pot and hash dealers cluster in a place called Pusher Street.

A taxi drops the wide-eyed Atlanta couple at Christiana's front gate since cars can go no further. Transportation inside is only on two wheels and two feet. Winding through curving streets shaped by ancient stonework, eventually they find Julie's address.

Before they have a chance to knock on her weathered door painted lavender, Julie rushes out to greet them warmly. She wears a full-length orange and red caftan. Silver bracelets of many cultures tinkle and jangle on both wrists. Her long, wavy white hair spirals in every direction. Ella can tell instantly she's a true eccentric and a woman of intensity.

"You made it. How fabulous that you came. Charlie, you're gorgeous. I'm your Aunt Julie. Ella, you're gorgeous too. Come in. Thank you so much for coming to see me."

"We've never been outside the U.S.," Ella tells her. "Everything's so different and cool already."

Julie serves hot chamomile tea and chewy, handmade oatmeal cookies. "It's good to nap now to acclimate to the new time zone," she suggests. After dinner, Julie promises to show them why she insisted they come. Ella and Charlie fall asleep easily in each other's arms, exhausted from the overnight flight. "Whatever this special gift is, I know it's going to be amazing," Ella whispers in his ear.

Several hours later, Charlie wakes up to the pungent aromas of cumin, coriander and turmeric simmering in Julie's kitchen. He lets Ella sleep a little longer then wakes her with gentle kisses on her forehead and along the graceful line of her neck. It feels delicious to wake gradually from faraway dreams. She's still drowsy, slowly registering his loving caress as she returns to consciousness. She feels more connected to Charlie than ever. He's the only familiar thing she knows in this new exotic world, still marveling how they found each other at all – years after their first chance meeting.

"What are you making?" Charlie asks Julie, stepping into the kitchen at dusk. "It smells fantastic."

"Oh good. It's an Indian style Mediterranean stew kind of thing with lentils, spices, sweet potatoes, couscous and prunes. It's different every time. Help yourself to appetizers."

A carved wooden tray is beautifully arranged with dried apricots and dates, salted cashews, stuffed grape leaves, cucumber and carrot sticks, three rolled joints and a handmade ceramic pipe filled with hash.

Once Julie's special guests enjoy their first bowl of nourishing stew, she gets down to it.

"Charlie, do you see and hear things others don't see? Do you feel vibrations and pick up energies others don't feel?"

The two young travelers look at each other with knowing smiles. Aunt Julie is reaching him. Charlie exhales from deep within his ribcage, thinking, *Does she get me? Can I be real with her? Maybe she can make sense of the mysteries I thought I'd never solve.*

"Of course, you do," Julie says, without needing an answer. "Our dad Ernest had it. Jill had it. Sometimes I have it. I knew it would accelerate even further with you, sweet Charlie. It's a gift of added perception and brain capacity."

She goes on, "I've smoked a lot of grass in my day, growing up in the 60s. I'm the one who first turned Ernest on. When you smoke pot with your dad day and night, it gives you license to smoke for the rest of your life. He had this manic intensity that I have too, and the pot mellows us out. Jill wasn't like that. She always had a natural calm.

"But now my lungs are almost shot, and the emphysema is killing me. At the same time, the lung cancer is spreading again — from all the damn cigarettes I smoked and probably from breathing too much smog in LA as a teenager."

"I'm so sorry, Julie," Ella says with genuine compassion.

"I don't care. I've had a good life. Living here is like being in an alternative universe. I'm sheltered from a lot of bullshit back in America. Like making every decision based on money. Everything is for the e-*CON'*-omy," stretching out the sound like it's a stinking dirty word. "American CEOs ignore the long-term effects of their short-sighted actions. Europeans have a more civilized approach. But let's not talk politics. Are you ready to receive my gift?"

"Sure," Charlie tells her.

Julie moves more slowly now as the pain returns. She bends down to the bottom drawer of an antique mahogany chest, lifting a large maroon velvet sack that seems heavy.

"I stole this from Jill's closet after her funeral. You were just one week old. Hank never knew about it."

At that moment, the front door opens. A tall, gentle man lets himself in. Though his face is leathered from decades of sun, and his thinning hair is etched in silvery whites and charcoal greys, his resemblance to Charlie is unmistakable. Astonishing. Spooky.

"This is my dear friend Stephan. He's the one you've been emailing with," Julie says.

"Stephan, say hello to Charlie and Ella. They made it! Stephan lives here with me now," Julie explains.

The guy seems strangely familiar to Charlie. "Thanks for all your help, Stephan. Great to meet you. Have we ever met before?" Charlie asks him.

"No, I don't think so, though I *did* know your mother many years ago," Stephan says.

A fragrant fire burns in a cobblestone fireplace in the center of the room. The orange flickers and popping crackles feel primeval, comforting, familiar.

"I was just about to give Charlie his gift," Julie tells Stephan. "Join us."

Sitting on the floor cross-legged, Aunt Julie faces Charlie. In silence, she pulls an enormous, jagged emerald the size of her hand from the pouch. It's a rough natural shape, faceted in irregular places. The shining green gem picks up the fire's amber glow, radiating a green-orange blend of eerie light. Ella and Charlie are transfixed.

Julie hands it to Charlie, their fingers touching. The transfer is made to the next generation.

"This magical jewel has been passed down for generations of our family," Julie explains to her only nephew.

She shares the family legend about a 12-year-old distant relative named Lilith who found it in the late 1800s while foraging for mushrooms in the tropical forests of Colombia, the source of the world's finest emeralds.

Little Lilith spots a corner of the rock jutting out from furry moss and decaying leaves. It sparkles with raindrops when the sun returns. She uses another rock to dig all around it to uncover its massive size, poking and scraping until her fingers bleed. She can barely lift the heavy gem but is determined to bring it home. Using every ounce of her strength, she pries it loose and carries it back to the village. She asks the clouds, *Why am I the lucky one to find this buried treasure? Why me?*

Her father explains the gem was determined to find *her* and "will bring luck for life." She believes him, growing up to be a wise leader and living longer than any of her peers.

Emeralds form gradually through a miraculous alignment of four elements fusing and bruising for 500 million years – beryllium, aluminum, silicon and oxygen.

Conditions in the underground veins must be just right. Since high temperatures and pressure levels increase deeper below the surface, the brew stews silently in the darkest darkness for millennia. Eventually, the veins cool enough for clear crystals to fuse like the irresistible chemistry between secret lovers.

If the beryllium contains traces of chromium, only then will the clear crystal transform to brilliant green.

Lilith's gem has remained in the family all this time, yet Julie only knows the names of recent relatives. "Ernest's mother Maria got it from her mother Sofija, a Lithuanian empress. Maria passed it to Ernest, the first man to own it. Ernest passed it to his firstborn, Jill. And now I have the privilege to pass it on to you, Charlie. Guard it carefully for the rest of your life."

Charlie is speechless, trying to sense what powers and secrets the price-less emerald might hold. The green rock feels so right in his hands.

"Thank you, Aunt Julie. What an incredible treasure."

Using her wisest goddess tone, Julie slowly goes on, dropping her voice an octave. There's more. "You and I are different from everyone else. We are *Homo splendens* – a new emerging species of *Homo sapiens*." She adds emphasis to the word splendens, rolling it around her tongue and throat, resonating like the lowest strings on a harp.

She pauses to give that thought time to sink in. Then Julie continues by describing an added layer of brain matter that hugs the surface of the substantia nigra – a tiny black speck in the brain that produces dopamine. The added brain matter is similar in size and shape to an infant's pinky finger, gently curving, slowly evolving over centuries.
Akin to the eyelash phase
of a thin crescent moon lunule
becoming brighter.

Charlie's brain has a larger add-on than any of his relatives and other splendens scattered around the planet.

"Now that the emerald is yours, you'll get pregnant. It holds some unex-plainable energies that stimulate birth. The baby will be a splenden. I'm sure of it," Aunt Julie says, breaking into a joyful, wrinkled smile.

Charlie and Ella look at each other as their eyes glaze with information overload, trying to understand. They both look to Stephan, hoping for an-swers. He calmly looks back, nodding, shrugging his shoulders. "We're all guided by forces larger than we can comprehend."

After the two couples talk late into the night, Charlie and Ella fall into bed, their minds crammed to overflowing.

"There's something odd about Stephan. Feels like I know him," Charlie whispers.

"I know what you mean. He seems familiar to me too," Ella confirms. "It's his eyes. But how would we know him?"

*   *   *

They spend several days with their elders, walking wooded trails on the island, getting to know each other and feeling at home.

One night, Julie overdoes it on wine and smoke, breaking down sobbing in an emotional apology to Charlie.

She's always been volatile, hiding behind a tough, outrageous exterior to over-compensate. Dyslexia was her downfall, a mysterious condition no expert could even name back in the '60s when she was in grade school struggling to read. Julie was obviously bright and articulate, yet written words, the alphabet and numbers made no sense to her.

She worked for a cutting-edge contemporary arts center in San Francisco after graduating art school there. Julie handled the public, and the complex, personal issues of temperamental artists, while her boss Carl handled the business end and everything else. They were pioneers in the California performance art and video scene, publishing respected magazines and two scholarly books. Carl even claimed he invented the first Internet, calling it The Well in the early '70s.

That's when she met Seth Simon, a rebel refugee from a wealthy New York family. Julie married the eccentric artist who was also defeated by dyslexia. Their tumultuous personalities clashed too often, leading to divorce just three years later. Thankfully, Julie received a few million in the settlement, allowing her to live well on her own terms.

"Please forgive me for not being part of your life," Julie tells Charlie as more tears run down her red-hot face. "I was absolutely devastated when my only sister died for no fucking reason. I couldn't face you. I had to run, first escaping to London, then Amsterdam, then finally landing here. I should have been there for you. I should have reached out sooner. I couldn't do it. I was too selfish and broken."

Charlie takes her hand. "I forgive you. Let's not have regrets. I'm grateful for this time together now. I love knowing someone from my real family."

Julie and Stephan look at each other and nod. That's the opening they've been waiting for to share one more shocking truth.

"It's time you know another family secret," Julie says hesitantly.

Ella reaches for Charlie's hand, holding it tight, thinking, *Oh God, now what?*

Stephan takes over. "Charlie, Hank is not your real father. I am."

Charlie's heart stops still. His whole body freezes. *What? How is this possible? Who the hell are you? I knew there was something about you . . .*

"I've been using the name Stephan here, but my real name is Grover. I loved your mother very much. I'm the one who planted the garden at your house."

His son's face turns ghost white. Ella is stunned. Julie holds her tongue, letting the unsettling news start to percolate.

"We're connected by blood," Grover goes on. "Now that we've met, I feel it so strongly. But Jill insisted we keep everything secret to not upset Hank. It really hurt. I lost my right to be your father. I missed the experience of being in your life. It's my deepest regret. I'm just hoping you can possibly forgive me and find a place in your heart for me now." He hangs his head, heavy with grief.

After a long silence, Charlie speaks. "Somehow this really makes sense. I love Hank. I thought *he* was my only family. Yet there's always been a distance between us. There's no physical resemblance, and he's not interested in the natural world. The minute I saw you, something felt familiar and right. Wow. I'm blown away. I *believe* you're my real dad. It's fantastic we can finally meet."

Grover stands up, stretching out his arms. Though Charlie is still frozen with shock, he tries to relax into his father's embrace, hugging him back. They finally let go and look into each other's faces for the first time, unable to unlock their gaze. Grover's eyes, though drooping and sad, are the same shade as Charlie's eye that's emerald moss green.

Charlie's cells align up and down his spine. A warm tingling in his arms and legs tells him he's found a missing key clicking into an unknown lock, freeing it open.

"I feel the blood connection too," Charlie assures him. "Something I've never, ever felt. I have so many questions for you."

"Let's take a walk," Grover suggests.

Julie and Ella are overcome by the sweet power of the heartfelt reunion. Both are beaming with big smiles of loving approval – one young, one old.

Walking out into the crisp night air, their steps are in sync. A three-quarter moon lights up the clear black sky. Charlie feels new valuable information pouring in.

"Can we be in each other's lives now?" Charlie asks.

"I want that more than anything," Grover answers right back.

"I'll have to get Hank to understand somehow," Charlie says.

"I can't erase the past," Grover tells him. "I made plenty of mistakes. My worst mistake was staying away from you for so long. Julie and I both abandoned you and we regret it terribly. We left you on your own with Hank. And he raised you well. All we can do now is to be there for you in the future. We want to know you and be supportive of all the amazing adventures still ahead of you."

They walk without speaking now, their feet crunching crisp, cold leaves. The night air smells delicious and clear.

"How has the garden matured?" Grover wonders.

"It's fantastic, Dad. I love that garden. I've learned so much from it. Can I call you Dad?"

"Of course. Please."

As they walk deeper into the woods, a huge owl calls out to the dark. Charlie stops walking and takes the opportunity to give Grover a gift. He focuses his mind on drawing the big bird closer. Soon a six-pound Eurasian eagle owl *(Bubo bubo)* floats to a landing on Charlie's outstretched arm.

Instinctively, Grover remains perfectly still. Both stare into the speckled bird's round eyes. Mars orangey-red with gigantic ebony-black pupils. Charlie gently strokes its back, showing his love and respect. The owl speaks to Charlie softly as if whispering.

"You have found a profound part of yourself.
Never lose this connection, Nature Boy.
Ancestors are precious fuel for moving forward.
Stay connected to your father. Always."

Since he's communicated with many birds by now, Charlie's getting the rhythm of their languages. They all impart life truths in concise, direct ideas.

"I hear you. I understand," Charlie whispers back.

Once its wisdom is passed on, the stunning henna-colored creature can return to his own family. Flexing strong wings, spanning six feet, he soars silently into the deep black night.

Grover is stunned, of course. His knees almost collapse under him from the unexpected close encounter. He's been holding his breath and can finally exhale.

"Owl gave me a beautiful message about you. He says you and I must stay connected always."

"You really are a force of nature, Charlie. I'm in awe of who you've become."

The bond between them is growing solid and strong. Both lives will be richer now that Grover's secret identity can be accepted openly.

A huge weight is lifted from Grover's mind. It feels like a brick wall he's been carrying on his chest is crumbling away. Spending time with his son is an intense mental and physical relief, filling his tired body with renewed energy and resolve.

Knowing who his real father is boosts Charlie's confidence. The puzzle pieces start to click into place, like untangling an unsolvable mystery. Sharing genes with a master horticulturist explains everything.

* * *

On Monday morning, Charlie visits mycology professor Frederik Jakobsen in the University of Copenhagen's biology department. Charlie set up the meeting in advance by email, sharing his mushroom experiments on bio-remediation in Nancy Creek. Jakobsen finds the data intriguing since he also works in this specialty, experimenting with Oyster mushrooms' potential to soak up pesticides and micro-plastic pollution in the Baltic Sea.

Over coffee, the almost retired professor is impressed with Charlie's abilities to grasp scientific intricacies. Since the kid also gets the more intangible, mystical properties of mushrooms, he decides to share his unpublished work-in-progress with the handsome young scientist.

For 20 years, Jakobsen, his colleagues and students have delved into the mind-expanding potential of the Psilocybin mushroom, testing concepts initially introduced by American ethnobotanist Terrence McKenna who died too soon of a brain tumor.

Their work is known as the Stoned Ape Theory, examining a fascinating time when apes evolved into *Homo erectus*, an almost human species in Africa, between two million and 700,000 years ago.

As gorillas and apes developed excellent foraging skills, they sought out the most nutritious and beneficial foods the forests offered. One satisfying protein source was succulent insect grubs found below the surface of cow dung. As our early ancestors learned to seek out dried cow manure, they also encountered the slender Psilocybin mushroom which only grows in that same warm environment. Inevitably, the apes were getting high on the psychedelic mushrooms.

The theory: Psilocybin triggered a growth factor in the brain that encouraged self-reflection, opening previously untapped neural paths to different ways of perceiving the world, enlarging the brain and stimulating its development to become the species we are today – *Homo sapiens*.

"That's when our brains suddenly doubled in size, an extraordinary increase with no real explanation," Jakobsen goes on. McKenna believed the newly enlarged brains were the source of art, language, religious ritual, shamanism, and expressive dance, prompting an unprecedented open mindedness in our *Homo erectus* ancestors. A dramatic evolutionary leap forward in creative thinking fired up.

Strong evidence also shows Psilocybin activated vast improvements in vision and enhanced sexuality.

Eating Psilocybin greatly improved eyesight, especially a function called edge detection which relates to peripheral vision. Once our early ancestors realized the mushrooms were giving them such a tangible benefit to forage and survive, they continued to eat them. If a plant can increase visual acuity, those who eat it will thrive better than those who don't.

Another substantial side effect was enhanced sensual desire and increased erections, resulting in more sex and more successful pregnancies. The mushroom eaters could outbreed the others.

While primates are known for their male-dominant hierarchies, Jakobsen's research reveals a different story. As recently as 40,000 years ago, the Psilocybin-eating colonies became polyamorous, choosing multiple sexual partners over monogamy. Professor Jakobsen contends the uninhibited, group sex had profound results. Male gorillas could no longer identify specific offspring as their own progeny.

Children now belonged to the entire clan which held societies together in even stronger communal bonds for thousands of years. Charlie is reminded of how forests and expanses of mycelium operate, collaborating with every tree around them to nurture large groups of neighbors, sharing nutrients among young and old.

Jakobsen admits it seems simplistic to place such evolutionary weight on one mushroom, yet there's a growing acceptance among international scientists that Psilocybin was likely a critical catalyst in human evolution, and worth further study.

In fact, scientists and psychiatrists are currently testing micro-doses of Psilocybin with patients as a long-lasting cure for depression, heroin addiction and cancer patients' fear of dying. Results have been remarkable, finally bridging the gap between pharmaceuticals alone and the need for spiritual, mind-expanding experiences which may be as essential for optimal health as diet and exercise.

"Absolutely fascinating," Charlie says once the professor's impassioned stories are through. Inside he's reeling over how this connects to Julie's theories about expanded brain capacity in their family. He's tempted to share her ideas with Jakobsen but it's too new to fully comprehend; he prefers to keep it to himself for now.

Charlie and Jakobsen promise to stay in touch.

*   *   *

Today is their last in Copenhagen. They have one more stop – an unparalleled, gourmet restaurant called Noma, voted the very best restaurant in the world for four years in a row. Their menu is like no other, reinterpreting ancient Nordic cuisine, using the freshest seasonal choices, often foraged from forests by owner and food pioneer Rene Redzepi.

Reservations must be made eight months in advance. The prix fixe tasting menu is expensive: $435 a person. Charlie and Ella don't expect to eat there. They go in the morning before the restaurant opens, hoping to meet someone on the kitchen staff who knows local plants and mushrooms.

Online menus show the chefs' commitment to locally grown, seasonal gems. Every night, dinner is a one-of-a-kind experience, never to be repeated. October through December is Game and Forest Season when "we serve everything we can get our hands on – a teal for two, a goose for four, leg of moose, reindeer tongue and wild duck," according to the online menu.

January through early June is Seafood Season, "the absolute best time for Scandinavian seafood from the ocean."

Vegetable Season is the end of June through mid-September when "we explore every edible aspect of the plant kingdom, cooking with what we find underground, above ground, near the water and in the trees, working closely with farmers and growing produce in our own urban farm and greenhouses."

Charlie and Ella find the unmarked restaurant, which recently moved not far from Julie's house on Christiania. A cluster of renovated brick buildings fits right into the landscape. They walk around to the back of the biggest one that feels like a huge, aging barn. The back door is wide open since it's a warm sunny day. Baskets brimming with rare mushrooms sit on blonde wooden countertops.

"Wow, those are the biggest Yellow Elanor morels I've ever seen," Charlie says to a young man unloading two more baskets from the back of a small pickup truck.

"You know the Yellow Elanor?" the young man asks. "I'm impressed. Few people know this one."

"We have the true morel, *Morchella esculenta,* growing wild in Atlanta, Georgia."

The three introduce themselves. Ella boasts that Charlie is an expert mycologist. "You must be," Ben smiles. "Have you ever tasted these?"

"Never," Charlie replies.

"Well, I was about to sauté a handful to see if they taste as good as last week's find. These are from a different wetland. You're welcome to have a taste. Relax in the garden near the pond. I'll find you."

Eventually, Ben returns with a plate of steaming Morels, simmered in handmade butter and sprinkled with fresh mint. Chewy, meaty, earthy, magnificent. Charlie and Ella thank him again and again for such an unexpected treat.

They even get a glimpse of tonight's dessert, being assembled by two young Danish women. It's a lemon pudding blend of pureed blueberries and walnuts, molded into a perfect circle, topped with large, roasted shiny black ants, surrounded by fresh green Wood sorrel.

"Someday we'll be back to experience a whole meal here," Charlie says to his easy-going partner.

"Another amazing experience to look forward to," Ella smiles back, taking his hand, fitting hers perfectly.

*   *   *

While Ella is alone in the guest room packing, Aunt Julie slips in and quietly closes the door.

"Darling, I feel compelled to share something. You need to know that *Homo splendens* are known for shorter life spans. Their death can come quickly and much too soon, like what happened to Jill," Julie tells her.

"Charlie seems solid and strong but be aware. And keep it to yourself. The best advice I can give is cherish every day you have with him. Fill your heart with gratitude for his incredible life. And know how fortunate he is to have a remarkable force like you by his side. I can't tell you how good I feel about meeting you both and knowing you have each other."

"We loved spending time with you, too," Ella says. "Charlie is my miracle man. I'm not letting anything happen to him. I'm sure we'll be together for a very long time."

"You will, Ella. Of course, you will."

Chapter 15 – Recalibrating After Copenhagen

Asarum splendens leaves with dwarf iris flowers

B ack in Atlanta, Charlie feels centered again, feet replanted in his cherished garden. Returning to his native habitat after opening to new perspectives in Europe rejuvenates his connection to his own landscape and the future.

Finding his real father is a treasure he never could have imagined. Blend that with Julie's *Homo splendens* theory that he's on the forefront of brain evolution. Both revelations strengthen his affinity for nature, and his abilities to tune to truths others can't grasp. It's becoming even easier to accept and embrace his rare powers.

He knows the word splendens from a plant in his garden, *Asarum splendens* in the ginger family. Its large heart-shaped leaves are variegated and showy. The second Latin word in a plant name often describes its appearance. Displaying splendor or magnificence.

Strange, speckled maroon flowers hide under the leaves of *Asarum splendens* in early spring, hugging the ground to attract earth-bound pollinators like slugs and small crawling insects.

Are the domed flowers cranial or vaginal? Or both?

Several plant names include the term splendens, often defined as glittering, glistening – and with the double meaning for intelligence – brilliant and bright.

Asarum splendens flowers

Charlie remembers there's also a deep purple mushroom with tiny tentacles named *Stemonitis splendens*.

*   *   *

While Charlie and Ella were away, a favorite wooded site on Wieuca Road was clear-cut. It's one Charlie thought would never be built on because it's so steep. A sign says 10 new homes will be crowded on the sloping site which sits directly above a tributary spilling into Nancy Creek nearby.

Charlie is livid that his neighbors seem clueless about thousands of species – from microscopic to big as beavers and bucks – who will be negatively impacted as they let the local landscape continue to deteriorate. This short-sighted development has got to stop.

After losing another neighborhood patch of forest and tapping into his heightened sense of who he is, Charlie is determined to step out from passive shadows and take action – directing his unique skills toward real change, perhaps on a global scale. Why wait?

His greatest fear is that the media and government authorities will discover him and turn his powers into a freak show. He promises Ella he is resolute to remain anonymous, always working secretly and silently behind the scenes.

It's comforting to know he can count on Ella and Grover as supportive collaborators and team players.

The next day, Grover emails his son. Sadly, the lung cancer finally took over and he lost Julie last night. Her last words were all about Charlie and Ella. Their visit gave her the closure she needed to die fulfilled, "knowing the family's legacy is in such capable hands."

As executor of Julie's will, Grover will arrive in Atlanta soon with papers Charlie must sign related to his aunt's estate.

There may be no other horticulturist who studied the stock market as Grover has. Thanks to early advice from a retired banker who volunteered with him at the Atlanta Botanical Garden, Grover invested small amounts in the '90s and early 2000s in emerging companies like Apple and Amazon. Plant and wait. Buy and hold.

As his modest portfolio split and soared, he reconnected with Julie 15 years ago while visiting London to tour famous gardens in the English countryside. She had just been awarded a $4 million divorce settlement. Crippled by her fear of numbers, she had no idea how to invest it. She trusted Grover completely, urging him to step in and take charge.

Taking risks with someone else's money made him uncomfortable, and yet he knew he could help her. Like planting a young tree and seeing into the future to visualize how large it will become, he was confident these companies had many years of healthy growth ahead. Investing, like letting trees grow, takes extreme patience.

Soon Charlie will have those unlimited resources to buy anything he needs for his subterranean interventions as an eco-activist.

*   *   *

Gentle rain crackles and drips from the tallest pines, making their soaked trunks a richer, darker brown. Pine needles are a lusher, saturated shade of green.

Charlie is relieved, thinking, *This rain is what the garden needs.*

But he's also in turmoil. Can he find words to break the shocking news to Hank that he's not his real father? It could trigger a breakdown since Hank is already emotionally fragile and weak.

This Sunday is Father's Day, an odd time to drop the bomb, but Charlie has to do it.

Their Father's Day tradition is to walk the grounds of the Jimmy Carter Presidential Library and sit by the soothing lake. Charlie is thinking: *Maybe if we're in a public place, Dad won't lose it or explode.* As they watch ducks float in the Japanese garden, Charlie clears his throat.

"Dad, I met Grover in Copenhagen. He's been living with Aunt Julie. This is hard to say, but he claims he's my real father and I believe him. Mom insisted he never tell me the truth. But now that I'm an adult, they thought I should know, and encourage me to accept that I have two fathers."

Hank is thinking: *That bastard! I knew it. How dare he? I sensed this all along but couldn't admit it. You and I were always close and yet so different. More like buddies than father and son, fending for ourselves without Jill. And you never looked like me.*

He wants to scream but controls his first emotional response. After a long silence, Hank finally says, "This may seem crazy, but I'm not surprised. It makes sense. I've loved you with everything I have and yet sometimes it feels like we come from different planets."

"What do you mean, Dad?"

"The way you communicate with nature. Your incredible magical powers to make plants grow. That doesn't come from me."

Charlie looks at Hank with compassion. He's thinking, *It must be hard for you to understand me sometimes.*

Charlie says, "I'll never stop being your son. Instead of two traditional parents, maybe I'm meant to have two fathers."

Charlie takes his dad's hand. In one cascading wave, the 40-foot *Japanese Kousa dogwood* tree in front of them, full of buds, flings wide open into hundreds of snowy-white blooms all at once, from the ground up to its crown.

Kousa dogwood

Without words, this is Charlie's way to assure the father who raised him that they're connected for life.

"You're too much, Charlie. That's beautiful."

*   *   *

As he begins to accept this unexpected blow, Hank decides to make a big change. For months, he's been feeling restless, unfulfilled and eager for something new.

Deeply proud of the son he raised, Hank's heart tells him to let go of any anger and give Grover his chance to know this extraordinary young man.

Hank resigns himself to see it as a sign to leave Atlanta and turn over the house and garden to Charlie. His architectural photography career is winding down anyway. He's been longing to return to his childhood home in Denver to be near his brothers and high school friends.

"I'll always be your dad," Hank tells Charlie.

"Of course you are. I'll never stop loving you."

While Hank is in Denver looking for an apartment, Grover returns for the first time to the Atlanta garden he planted 25 years ago.

The young trees and shrubs have matured into tall, lush specimens – each distinct texture and shape layering one upon another to achieve the dense, miniature forest he imagined on every inch of his former lover's property.

Grover gave life to hundreds of rare plants that are now reaching their potential under Charlie's loving care. Both father and son played their roles in sustaining the beauty that's become a one-of-a-kind botanical wonder. Echoing the structure of old-growth forests with tall canopy trees, understory trees, lower layers of blooming shrubs and collections of unusual ferns, perennials and ground covers hugging the bottom layer. The place is a soothing natural retreat – in stark contrast to the neighbors' predictable Kelly green lawns.

Unlike his neighbors, Charlie lives simply, close to nature. He finds pleasure in random phenomena like fast-moving rain clouds, layered dark gray on white. In sensual shapes of flower buds a few days before spreading open. Or intricate black and white patterns of coded dashes and dots on a Downy woodpecker's back. These are the real jewels of life that feed his imagination, bringing joy and fulfillment.

Lycoris radiata buds about to open

He has no need for material possessions, fancy restaurants, designer clothes or luxury cars. He knows genuine riches have no price.

Yet Grover has some shocking news.

"Your Aunt Julie loved to surprise and provoke. That was always her style," Grover explains. "Perhaps her biggest shocker yet is what she left to you in her will. You're inheriting her entire estate worth about $85 million."

"Me?" Charlie asks incredulously. The unlikely multi-millionaire never saw this coming.

"Are you serious, Dad? What will I ever do with so much money?"

"You have plenty of time to think about it, Charlie. She knows you'll be thoughtful and find ways to put it to good use. It's one more tool to complement your talents. Use it to advance causes that matter to you and Ella."

Chapter 16 – The End of Amazon.com

Jeff Bezos is the richest man on the planet, supposedly worth $200 billion. He rewrote the book on Internet sales, starting with a modest $300,000 loan from Mommy and Daddy.

Now that Charlie is a major shareholder of Amazon.com, inherited from Aunt Julie, he feels entitled to steer the company's priorities in a different direction. He's determined to hold Amazon.com true to its name and rescue the irreplaceable Amazon rain forest before it's too late.

Although Bezos donates millions to charities working to end cancer and homelessness, he's spent billions on the uncertainties of space exploration. Charlie thinks that's crazy; protecting the planet we have makes more sense. His goal is to move Bezos away from his obsession with high-tech solutions and focus on timeless, analog ideas at ground level. He knows one of the most effective ways to do that is to preserve tropical forests still standing especially in Columbia, Brazil, Ecuador, Peru and Costa Rica, and plant billions of new trees to enhance life-giving powers of existing forests as the source for countless undiscovered cures and medicines. Home to millions of species of flora and funga still unknown to humans, and a vital source of pure oxygen.

Determined to remain behind the scenes and anonymous, Charlie crafts a plan to infiltrate the multibillionaire's dreams, sending silent messages to wake him up. While Bezos sleeps, Charlie will pack his brain with unforgettable, ominous dreams too real to ignore.

To ensure success, Charlie figures he better be physically close to Bezos when trying to alter his subconscious mind. He learns the Amazon CEO will be at his Blue Origins headquarters in two weeks in the remote town of Van Horn, Texas to observe another test rocket launch.

Just 70 miles away is the quirky town of Marfa, a hip cultural center with prestigious artist-in-residence programs, cutting edge galleries, and film and music fests that attract art lovers from around the world. Ella has always wanted to go, so he books a room at a Marfa resort for a week, close enough to Bezos while keeping his distance.

As Charlie and Ella relax in their comfortable hotel bed, Charlie directs his thoughts to pierce Bezos' subconscious like a handmade spear racing to its target. The first dream takes shape.

Bezos and his young son Aidan drift through the Amazon jungle in a canoe. Their guide is an indigenous shaman who carries generations of wisdom passed through unwritten languages. Father and son are completely in his hands, reluctantly trusting him with their lives. Why am I here? Bezos wonders.

He is clearly out of his element.

Thick gnarled tree limbs, dripping with humid rain, puncture the dark water with black velvet shadows. Shrill sounds are everywhere as howler monkeys scream above their heads, leaping across the canopy. Orange and blue Macaw parrots squawk and shriek as they swoop near their faces. Tremendous bullfrogs click and croak, staring back with liquid green eyes floating on the river's surface. Hundreds of insects are woven into every inch of the strange, steamy world. Their songs rise to crescendos at ear-piercing volumes, then shudder to a lull before the cycle repeats and winds back up again. It starts to pour. Then the volume of drenching rain doubles, drowning out any other sounds. It pours even harder.

Bezos has no idea how they got here, feeling vulnerable, scared and now soaking wet. Yet he wants to appreciate the richness of life swarming around him. They spot a family of exotic ocelots lurking on the shore. They're magnificent.

Aidan tries to catch a frog by reaching into the river. Instead, he attracts a giant poisonous eel who digs its fangs deep into the child's hand. Young Bezos screams out in agony. Aidan's right thumb dangles from a single strand of muscle.

His father panics and is losing it, asking himself, "What am I doing here? How can we get out? No helicopter could find us or even land. There's no cell service anyway. Is this how my life ends? Does Aidan have to die with me? It's too soon. I'm not ready to die."

The usually confident executive is terrified to the bone.

But the shaman remains calm, reaching into his pouch for a soothing oil distilled from the roots of Jewel weed. He grabs the boy's arm and rubs the tincture into the wound. The bleeding stops immediately, and the kid finally stops crying. Father and son watch in awe as the wound shrinks to nothing within seconds. The thumb is seamlessly reattached; the pain vanishes.

Without words, the shaman lets Bezos know his forest is full of powerful cures like this. A loud, constantly ticking clock gets closer as if time is running out. Running out on his own life and his company. And running out for life on the planet.

Surrounded by this dense jungle full of mystery, Bezos is struck by the absurdity of his 10,000-year clock project, a symbolic icon to "long-term thinking" being built in the mountains of West Texas.

Though invisible, Charlie has dropped into the canoe with them, taking even closer control of Bezos' mind, bending it to embrace unexpected perspectives. Instead of focusing on profits and shareholder returns, Bezos realizes, "It's up to me to save the Amazon." Charlie plants this simple chant in Bezos' brain, repeating over and over.

"The Amazon is an irreplaceable living treasure, not just the name of my company. I have the power to save the Amazon forests. I can do this."

The shaman, who is also Charlie, keeps staring into Jeff Bezos' brain, urging him to realize how many nature-based medicines and cures are possible only if those plants are saved from extinction. The shaman digs even deeper into Jeff Bezos' mind, spilling a subtle golden light into his eye sockets, directing him to take action.

"It's up to me to save the Amazon. It's up to me . . ."

*   *   *

Bezos is clearly distracted by last night's unsettling dream. He's haunted by the question, *How many undiscovered medicines and solutions are lost forever as the Amazon's forests are cleared for short-term profit and grazing cattle?*

Two nights later, his dreams send him back to the jungle.

He's floating again on a remote and narrow tributary of the Amazon River. This time 25 canoes are overflowing with people. They're a mix of local, brown-skinned natives and sun-deprived pale faces from Seattle. The white people are frantically looking down at dead smart phones, desperate for a signal that will never come.

Cool damp forest shadows abruptly switch to blaring full sun. Riverbanks have been recently decimated – cleared of every tree and trace of vegetation. Cheap beef processing factories are being built by Chinese workers. Natural sounds and songs are gone. Only hammering and electric chain saws screech in the empty landscape.

Bezos is alone in his canoe now without a guide, helpless and lost. At his feet is another leather pouch. Inside are smooth black seeds, slightly larger than watermelon seeds with intricate spotted brown patterns. He realizes they're the last seeds of some extinct plant that holds great potential to rejuvenate neurons in the human brain.

There's also something wrapped in a shiny green leaf tied with twine. Bezos opens the package and holds a dried, shriveled pink mushroom in his hand. As he stares at it, the rare fungus starts pumping with golden light like a beating heart, breathing with life, glowing with an otherworldly brightness. Obviously, this iridescent mushroom is a cure for something too, but what? He's determined to escape with his life and preserve these valuable natural treasures.

In the distance, large groves of tall trees begin to topple, hundreds at a time. Their roots forced to give up the fight and let go. Bezos shivers with fear as the disaster is unfolding – completely beyond his control.

In his morning shower, he's still staggering. Every dream has more vibrant colors and 3D images than he's ever experienced. *Why am I dreaming about the Amazon forest? These dreams are so damn real.* He's flooded with new resolve to change his personal and corporate priorities.

*   *   *

The multibillionaire becomes obsessed with the Amazon, a place he's never seen. Avoiding any public announcement, he quietly clears his calendar for the month of May. He confides in *Washington Post* writer Scott Mooney who travels there often, writing about local customs including the potent natural medicine Ayahuasca.

Jeff Bezos is clearly at a life crossroad, compelled to change directions. Even though Ayahuasca is not recommended as a one-time experience, he's ready to experiment with the ancient rain forest ritual. He trusts Scott to arrange a private, personalized trip with the most knowledgeable shaman guide – Emilio Gonzales, a well-respected, 55-year-old Peruvian who has secretly introduced other elite Americans to the mind-altering hallucinogen.

Every shaman has his own recipe for the powerful drink that blends vines, flowers, leaves and bark from the psychedelic shrub *Psychotoria viridis* and sometimes even chemicals scraped from the skin of certain frogs and fish. Gonzales requires Bezos to alter his diet weeks in advance and be prepared for disastrous reactions.

*   *   *

Tonight is the night. Surrounded by a breathtaking magenta sunset, hesitantly, Jeff Bezos forces the bitter potion down his throat, wincing and gagging. Soon he's vomiting violently, his intestines churning inside out. He regrets his decision to drink the murky brown magic, wondering how he can escape.

As he gives in to his suffering and self-pity, a light breeze slowly creeps under his skin. The horrible body tremors finally subside. Somehow, he's standing on a rocket launching pad surrounded by the soaking wet jungle. Before he can enter the rocket, his brain bursts open. Jewel-toned patterns shaped like ice crystals explode through both ears and his mind lifts off, hovering 10 feet above ground looking down at his crumpled body, relieved to be free of it.

His mind soars higher, flying above the tree canopy into the ebony night. Without a rocket, without clothes or oxygen, he zooms higher and faster into another galaxy swirling with orange and silver stars. Every regret, every mistake he's ever made flies through him like speeding meteors colliding with his heart then ricocheting out to distant stars, allowing him to let them go. For five hours, he floats in pure black outer space, empty, cold and utterly alone.

He's sure he's venturing way too far, doomed to drift in this nothingness forever – never able to return to Earth, or to see colors and light, or to hug his kids. In the bleak loneliness, he feels a tremendous weight lift from inside every cell, being cleansed and rearranged in the roaring blackness.

*   *   *

He returns home as a new man with a radically fresh perspective. His drive to keep growing the business is over – he's certain he's taken the company as far as he can. It's time to liquidate his shares and turn the assets into something real – a force for healing the planet. He'll apply his lifelong business acumen to create far-reaching high-tech systems for new endeavors that mimic and enhance natural systems.

Instead of gambling billions and abandoning planet Earth to explore outer space, over the next five years Bezos personally buys hundreds of thousands of acres of South American rain forest, placing tight restrictions on their development forever. He creates thousands of high-paying local jobs for tree planting teams to replant and nurture native trees by the millions, pledging resources to keep the effort going at an aggressive pace for the next 250 years.

Honoring Amazonian tradition, he places indigenous women in charge. Several offshoot businesses are formed, using native fruits, nuts, mycelium and seeds to make healing oils, tinctures, creams and other handmade products that promote health. Taking advantage of Amazon's distribution networks, they're made available globally. People are hungry for nature-based products like these.

The concept is extremely popular with citizens around the world who affectionately name the protected wildlife sanctuaries the Bezos Forests. Each year, the bold strategy captures vast amounts of carbon, halting decades of destruction. Teams of ethnobotanists and ethnomycologists are well paid to catalog and collect rare plants and mushrooms for further study. Climate scientists are employed on every continent to complement tree plantings where they live, measure results and devise new ways to keep reducing greenhouse gas emissions.

Bezos also announces that in addition to the Amazon project, he'll use his fortune to kickstart an intensive effort to fund renewable energy sources to slow climate change. A radical pivot from coal and fossil fuel.

One of Charlie's dreams is realized.

Note: This fantasy was written one year before the $10 billion Jeff Bezos Earth Fund was established in February 2020 to address the climate crisis.

Chapter 17 – Imagining Myco-Town

It's a year since Aunt Julie's passing. Charlie, Ella and Grover are a brainstorming hurricane. Hanging out as a threesome, creative ideas are flowing. *How do we maximize Julie's gift? Where do we plant roots in rich dark soil to make the $85 mill mature into a Mother Tree? Feeding the forest and multiplying her influence.*

Some of their ideas are
- Partner with Paul Stamets, one of the world's leading mycologists turned entrepreneur.
- Launch a national education campaign for homeowners to stop spraying and watering lawns and replace them with native trees, shrubs and wildflowers to benefit birds, insects and air quality.
- Provide grants to educator Doug Tallamy, who envisions backyards across the country as one continuous nature corridor and the nation's largest park.
- Visit the Seven Wonders of the World, especially Machu Picchu, Hanging Gardens of Babylon and the Great Pyramid of Giza to gain insight and wisdom from ancient cultures.
- Return to Copenhagen to eat at Noma every night.
- Visit Stonehenge during a full moon.
- Buy real estate in and around Atlanta to protect the tree canopy and prevent the last remnants of forest from being developed.
- Establish an advisory team of Georgia's best ecologists. Encourage them to collaborate with each other instead of competing for funding. Provide start-up capital for their joint projects.
- Travel the world for a year, searching for impressive young companies working with mushrooms in new ways especially in The Netherlands, Denmark and Israel. Invest in their projects.

"What if there's some great idea we haven't thought of yet?" Charlie asks Ella. "It would be fun to open our minds to more possibilities. Want to drink some mushroom tea and see what happens?"

"Have you done it before?" Ella asks.

"I have."

"Tell me more. What does it feel like?"

"It's like stepping into a new dimension, another way of thinking. It's subtle and smooth since it's organic, not synthetic with hard edges. You tune in to different wave lengths. For me, there's always a sensual rush that pumps through my veins, heightening all of the senses especially touch. You'll love it, Ella."

"Hmmm. That sounds really good, Charlie. If you're with me, I know I'll be safe. Our own private party."

Charlie is inspired to brew a special blend for his favorite person in the world. Native Smilex vines are at the right stage when soft, reddish tips emerge. Clip three. Vitamin C-rich Chickweed is also popping up. Pull three handfuls. Add Lion's Mane mushroom tincture and fruit for added brain clarity. Call Nick Juno (an acquaintance and Psilocybin connoisseur who collects the finest specimens from cow pastures at his family farm outside Calhoun). Chop three fresh, large clumps. Add the three-lobed leaves and springy tendrils of Passionflower vine for flavor and passion.

After simmering his brew for three hours, the honey-colored elixir is poured into a jumbo glass pickle jar, covered tightly, and left outside in the sun for three days. Sun soaking melds and intensifies each ingredient, boosted by the healing energies of solar power.

The venue is crucial and sets the tone of any trip. Of course, they'll be outdoors in nature.

They decide on Lula Lake, a little-known spot near Chattanooga, Tennessee. With miles of walking trails and a crystal-clear lake, the backdrop will be welcoming and serene.

As they leave early for the two-hour drive, both marvel at the Kousa dogwood blooming like crazy near the front door.

Planted by Grover as a five-foot-tall experiment, it's loaded with thousands of creamy white flowers. The extra rain, cooler temperatures and 25 years of maturity give the towering tree an otherworldly glow.

Charlie snaps this photo of Ella silhouetted by the blinding white blooms, engulfed by the tree's exquisite abundance.

Kousa dogwood in peak bloom

They don't eat much, a few boiled potatoes and roasted broccoli so they can fully absorb the tea.

Once they find a shady spot on the lake, Charlie pours the enchanted brew into handmade ceramic cups. They toast to an enlightening journey together, today and forever.

"Drinking a cup of sunshine," Ella says, smiling with love, looking straight into his two-toned eyes.

He warns she may feel nauseous at first but then a surge of euphoria will take over.

A few hours later, they're both beaming with perpetual smiles, laughing out loud. At everything. Squirrels climbing. Bullfrogs croaking. Bumble bees buzzing and drinking nectar.

Arms linked, following trails, their bodies fuse as they walk, hips attached.

Ella's feeling overly sentimental and blurts out, "I still can't believe I found you, Charlie. You're the man for me."

"I know I am. I've loved you for centuries. You look like a goddess from ancient Greece reincarnated so we can be together right here right now."

She grabs his hand and pulls him close. Kisses are more delicious than ever. Lips are ripe mango smooth, gliding toward a hidden cave inside each other's minds. With eyes closed, Ella soars through galaxies, floating weightless, completely free.

Pulling away from his burning embrace, she shouts, "I'm flying above the mountains. I'm looking down at a Native American village. It's snowing. I'm caught in a blizzard! But it's not cold. Everything feels fluffy and soft, covered in snowflakes like white frosting, sparkling in the sunlight."

"I like it. Go with it," he says. "Feel it."

Ella tunes in to her inner wisdom, letting inhibitions go, letting go of limits and time. She feels feather-light, joyful and complete, as if she can jump from cloud to cloud by simply imagining the sensation.

Under a protected hickory branch, Charlie spots a low-hanging cocoon. He guides her closer, moving slowly so they won't be noticed. The translucent sac rips open from the bottom as the butterfly's black and white spotted body shakes free, oozing out gradually. They are here at exactly the right moment.

Ella is awestruck, her mouth wide open. She can hardly believe what she's seeing. The tea gives her added concentration to stare intently at the new life emerging. A fresh start. It seems the metamorphosis is happening expressly for their pleasure. The butterfly's wet wings unfold in jerking motions; its long legs hold tight to the home it is about to abandon.

"That orange!" Ella exclaims. "It's so vivid and delicious." Her own body feels in sync with the young butterfly's new body, stretching and reaching to take flight. The sun dries and warms its new wings. They flatten and flutter and suddenly she's off.

"That was incredible," Ella says. "Thank you for finding that! I don't know how you do it."

She extends her own long arms, mimicking the Monarch's wings, flapping, reaching and smiling from within.

Charlie's trip is all about her. To the guy whose existence is nurtured by nature, at this moment, he is captivated by Ella's looks. At age 28, her beauty is at its peak. The first signs of aging have already begun, though will remain invisible on the surface for years.

He chants to himself *Ella Bella Wella. Ella Wella Bella.* The words sound like bells ringing. He can't take his eyes off her trim waistline, the curves of her hips, the light in her eyes. He's thinking, *I'll never forget this moment. Frozen in time. Us together. Hopefully for a lifetime.*
I want to remember you exactly
like
this

Hours go by and Charlie and Ella are exhausted and invigorated at the same time after such intense workouts for their brains. Lying on a blanket, they hold each other, drifting into dreams, resting before driving back to Atlanta.

Once they're home safely, Ella falls into bed and doesn't get up until noon, feeling recharged and changed.

* * *

Ella says, "I keep thinking about that village I saw. They had a purpose. They had valuable knowledge that no one else had. It was a safe place where they could live and think differently."

Charlie realizes her imaginary tribe could be a clan of expert mushroom growers, cultivating and preparing indigenous fungi for optimal health. Dedicated to knowing everything possible about mushrooms.

"Could we bring people together to live and breathe mushrooms?" Charlie asks her.

She nods gently. Simultaneously, they both begin to see the possibilities. An intentional community like this could have an impact. On medicine. On diet. On ecology. On a global scale.

Because of Charlie's lifelong passion for mushrooms' potential, he knows the mysteries they hold can change the health of the planet, perhaps change societies. A powerful concept is taking shape. **Myco-Town**.

To support the innovative work of his mycologist friends and other bright scientists they don't know yet, Charlie and Ella can build and manage a protected community devoted to every aspect of funga. Young mycologists and their families can live together, grow mushrooms, conduct research and be fully supported in their experiments. A safe place where high-level research will yield groundbreaking scientific evidence now being pursued with limited resources. Growing mushrooms and sharing their lives in a secluded Georgia forest, their discoveries will advance more quickly than working separately in labs and universities scattered around the world.

No other long-term research community like this exists anywhere. By living together, these brilliant minds will benefit from each other's experiments in a collaborative synergy.

New, inexpensive medicines to challenge the pharmaceutical establishment will be developed. New products like leather for clothing, biodegradable packaging far superior to Styrofoam and plastic, and sturdy building materials will change the paradigm. Myco-Town inventions will improve the natural world, not deplete it.

Ella drafts a mission statement. Her latest version reads:
Myco-Town is a collaborative community of mycologists searching for mushroom-based solutions to enhance and protect life on Earth.

Results will be made widely available, without pressure to maximize profit. Every new food, medicine and product will be affordable and accessible aiming to disrupt Big Pharma, the American Medical Association, the construction and packaging industries and the broken agriculture industry. Think mushroom-based health drinks and high-protein, vitamin-packed snacks for starters.

Another important specialty will take existing research on Oyster mushrooms to the next level. Clean, bio-remediation projects that neutralize toxic chemicals in soil and water will be put into practice on a massive scale.

The trio spends all summer looking at properties about two hours north of Atlanta. Grover finds a promising 300-acre forested parcel in the foothills of the Blue Ridge Mountains surrounded by Chattahoochee National Forest near the tiny town of Tiger, Georgia. He invites Charlie and Ella to scout it out on this glorious cool morning.

As they drive up the steep unpaved entry road, they're immediately struck by the high-quality of the mature forest punctuated with towering Beech, Tulip poplar, Slippery elm, White and Red oak. Opening the car windows, it's like breathing emerald.

While picnicking at the base of a huge Tulip poplar, Charlie spots the prized Morel mushrooms. He wanders off alone hoping for more.

Architectural shapes of a Morel mushroom

The temperature rapidly heats up as buttery light emanates from inside the trunk of another 200-year-old Tulip poplar. A thumping heartbeat becomes audible. Charlie can see with x-ray vision watching water and carbon dioxide shooting upward, pulsing through the tree's arteries like blood. Shimmering liquids and gases swirl in silvers and golds.

He watches new cells grow in the thin cambium layer below the bark. He listens to sugars descend through sun-soaked leaves above, shooting down the trunk as they absorb and feed roots, joining hands with fungal filaments below the loamy soil.

For the first time, he realizes ridges on the tree's bark are parallel lanes of a highway, directing rainwater from the sky to flow down the trunk's exterior, aiming it right to the roots, watering every cell evenly along the way.

It's a stunning show lighting up a large patch of fresh Morels below. Charlie feels the magic in this place already. Then the mighty tree starts to move, even without a trace of wind, curving its entire body slowly and deliberately toward him, bending down as its huge leafy crown sweeps the ground. At snail speed, the tree speaks.

"This is your n e w   g a r r r d e n.

We ee
　　　w a n t　　y o o o o o u
　　　　　　　　　　　　h e r e.
W e e　ee　e
　　　n ee e　ee e d
y o u u ur r
　　　　　　h e l p.
W e e e
 h a vvv e
　　　b e e nn n n
w aaa a i t i nn nn gg g
f o r
　　　y oo ou."

Charlie grabs one of the tree's thick limbs, caressing it, respecting it, listening with compassion to its language.

"I've been searching and waiting for you too," Charlie whispers. "We'll build a new model for living lightly on this land. Valuable discoveries will be made here from our hard work."

His imagination scans the full web of life – miniscule microbes, seeds and insects, reptiles, mammals, tall trees, mountain peaks and oceans, each one responding to myco-solutions, unlocking mysteries still to be revealed.

The enormous tree twists and shivers like a horse shaking its mane in agreement. Gradually, it springs back, returning to the upright stance it has held for centuries.

The search is over. When Charlie catches up with Ella and Grover, he's smiling. "I think we've found our place."

By the end of the week, Grover quietly puts the property under contract, offering to pay in full without a mortgage. It's only $1,500,000.

Next, he tracks down an old friend who once lived in Atlanta. Pablo Castilla was an imaginative architect back then. The octogenarian is still designing stunning homes. Oil painting is another passion. Jill wrote the catalog for his biggest one-man show at Millennium Gate Museum 30 years ago.

Grover challenges him to draft plans for modest yet elegant, eco-friendly, sunlight-filled dwellings. He imagines them in clusters on a hilltop, establishing Myco-Town's first housing. Building blocks made from mushrooms – hard as concrete – will shape their exteriors.

Scientists in their 20s and 30s will start families here so children can grow up immersed in nature – unplugged, independent and grounded. One or both parents will grow mushrooms for research. There will be plenty of surplus to sell at farmers' markets, gourmet restaurants and online. Eventually, first-class laboratories and small manufacturing plants will open.

Ella wants to add an art gallery and concert venue for residents and visiting artists, encouraging scientists to pursue their artistic sides. She also envisions fascinating classes for the public on appreciating mushrooms' essential roles in every ecosystem.

It's a long-range enterprise that will sustain itself over time. Discoveries and inventions made here will generate millions of dollars, reinvested to keep the community viable for at least seven generations. The concept originates with the Iroquois, native to upstate New York, who made important decisions only if they would benefit their children seven generations into the future. The Cherokee people who once lived here also took the long-term view when using nature's finite resources.

One more key player is recruited to join the team. Hank has a first cousin named Denise Remington whose specialty is incubating entrepreneurial ideas on a global scale. She's raised millions from venture capitalists for several international startups and understands complex patent and intellectual property laws. Denise suggests each scientist will own their discovery and benefit financially as an individual, while a fair percentage of their profit will return to the Myco-Town Foundation.

In their first meeting, Ella is impressed with Denise's business acumen and personal style. She sees Denise as an influential mentor.

Charlie believes in the concept so strongly that he's decided to invest his entire fortune in Myco-Town. He establishes an endowment fund, so every aspect will remain well maintained to his high standards.

Bowl of Morels from the new property

Confident that Ella's strengths will complement his, they're getting more comfortable with the idea of being life partners in business, as well as partners in love.

He also writes his first will, reserving $7 million for Ella personally. "I want to make sure she's taken care of in case anything ever happens to me," he tells Grover.

Chapter 18 – A New Species

Charlie wakes up knowing today will be his last. It makes no sense but suddenly he's very weak, fading as quickly as a fragile Mayapple flower. He's only 30.

As progress at Myco-Town is moving forward beautifully, it's too soon to die – yet an inner voice assures him a significant outcome will follow.

He's thinking of his mother Jill's mysterious death six days after his own life began. *Maybe Homo splendens die young. Though I've learned to communicate with trees, it doesn't mean I'll have their same long life span.*

His first instinct is to reach for Ella. She slipped out early for a 7:30 yoga class. Lying in bed, feeling his life force waning, he hears her key at the front door. There's no time to ease into the shocking news. He has to let her know now. This is likely their last day together.

"Sweetheart," he calls out, working hard to keep his voice strong.

"Good morning, Sleepyhead. You're still in bed?"

"Come close, Ella. I have to tell you something that's very hard to say."

"What is it, gorgeous one?"

"Something's happening to me. My life is fading fast. I know the reason will be clear later, but it's over. I'm dying. I can't explain it. I guess my work is done. The hardest part is leaving you alone too soon." His voice trails to a sad whisper. His eyes are moist, holding back tears.

"Charlie, what are you talking about? It's just the flu or a bad cold." She touches his forehead, hoping for a fever – desperate for an explanation. His forehead is cool, too cool. Her heart locks up as if a dagger is piercing through it.

She's thinking: *He would never talk like this if he weren't sure. Is this what Aunt Julie warned me about?*

"Charlie, you can't leave me now." Her eyes fill with tears too. "I'm not 100% positive, but I might be pregnant. I was going to tell you any day. You can't die now. I need you more than ever. You have to hold on. For the baby."

They clasp hands, grasping tight. "You're pregnant? That's fantastic, Ella."

He tries to sit up so he can pull her close but doesn't have the strength, falling back down into the pillows. After a few breaths, he whispers, "I'm so happy about our baby. This is how I'll live on in the next generation after all."

He's thinking: *My knowledge will live through our baby. My spirit can cycle back in rivers that never stop flowing. In planets that keep orbiting and roaring through space. In thousands of seeds the forest drops year after year. In mountains that never fall.*

"Let's go to Arabia Mountain today and celebrate," he says.

"Baby, please let me call Dr. Tinanoff," Ella pleads.

"NO! I want to transition in peace. No doctor can help me. I don't want anyone to try to save me. They can't. Let me have my last day with you."

She doesn't want to fight. She has to give in.

"Of course, Love. If that's what you want to do," she whispers. Every cell in her body tightens, heavy as cement. Her world is collapsing. She feels trapped in a cold dark cave with no exit.

Charlie is too weak to make it to the mountaintop. They return to the hidden patch of forest where they made love in the pouring rain, solidifying their lifelong commitment to each other.

Ella is thinking: *Is our love too powerful to sustain itself in this world? Can it really be ending already? Why do I have to accept this?*

Back home, as the sun sets dark grey and burnt orange, Charlie can barely speak. He reaches for her hand to pass along his final thought. "Tell our baby Mother Nature is the greatest force. The greatest artist and designer. The greatest scientist. Studying and caring for nature is everything."

Those are his last words as he crawls back into bed.

Ella prepares his favorite meal of Shiitake, avocado and wild caught salmon. He only eats a few bites.

She joins him under the covers. Shattered and terrified, Ella realizes this could be their last night. Of course, she can't sleep. All she can do is express her infinite love by kissing and caressing his exquisite body as it wilts and fades before her eyes. She slows her breathing, synchronizing with his, hesitant and faint. Around 3:00 am, Ella finally drifts into a dream for a few hours. That's when Charlie lets go, passing into another realm.

When she comes to, her beloved Charlie is gone. She hugs him tightly for hours, sobbing in disbelief, helpless. *How can his miraculous life be over? Why do I have to endure this excruciating pain?*

All she has left are her remarkable memories of being together.

*   *   *

The green burial takes place on land owned by the monastery in the Arabia Mountain National Heritage Area – one of the few sites in Georgia allowing bodies to decompose as naturally as the Cherokees did. Charlie's body is wrapped in white linen and placed directly in the earth so his nutrients and wisdom can recycle without embalming fluid or shiny casket. Ella tosses in a few of his favorite plants – *Asarum splendens,* Epimedium and Morel mushrooms.

The unmarked grave sits in a sun-drenched meadow surrounded by the poplars, dogwoods and pines he loved. Ella is there every morning, talking to him, asking for the strength to go on without him, floundering for direction.

On the seventh day, the grave looks different. Crenulated, greenish-blue mushrooms she's never seen before are popping up. Another week later, the mushroom mat has expanded tremendously, taking over half the grassy meadow.

She smiles for the first time in weeks. "It's Charlie," she says out loud. Ella collects several handfuls of the mushroom in a paper bag, thinking she will ask their mycologist friend Jordan Sparer to run DNA sequencing out of curiosity.

Within days, Jordan texts: *Call me right away. You're not going to believe this.*

Jordan ran the DNA tests three times to confirm the crazy results. "I think this is a completely unknown new species," he says excitedly. "It's unbelievable."

He explains why this mushroom is like no other. It has DNA from about 10 very different fungal species in addition to DNA all its own. "This could be an incredible new discovery. Some kind of miracle mushroom," Jordan tells her.

That evening, Jordan and his friend George Baron visit Ella and Grover to share their findings in person. George is even more experienced in analyzing fungal DNA.

The two young scientists are awestruck. In 400 million years of fungal evolution, such a potent, all-purpose organism like this has never been discovered. They explain how this new species has the same properties as Lion's Mane, known for rebuilding neurons in the brain. It also has DNA from the Chaga and Cordyceps which are proving beneficial in curing cancer. It has a delicate hint of the psychoactive ingredients in Psilocybin. But that's not all. It's part Oyster mushroom, high in vitamin D and zinc, essential elements rarely found in other foods.

"And as you already know, the Oyster is also excellent for myco-remediation able to soak up toxins like plastic and oil spills in the ocean, and poisonous pesticides on land.

"So what we're saying is this thing is probably delicious to eat, can be a powerful medicine, gives the perfect high, is loaded with hard-to-find vitamins and nutrients needed for good health *and* can easily break down chemicals and pollution," George says, raising his voice with delight. "There's never been a hybrid like this. Never."

Jordan adds, "Since you discovered it, Ella, you have the privilege of naming it."

Ella and Grover look at each other with knowing smiles. The rare bird of a man they loved so profoundly now gives the world a superb, unprecedented gift.

"We had to lose him for this super species to emerge," Ella finally says. "I'm as amazed as you both are. My heart is racing." *My heart is aching, missing him so much.*

*   *   *

While most mushrooms only live for a few days, Charlie's mushroom patch lasts for weeks, rain or sun. Jordan and George collect the spores and easily grow its mycelium in sterile greenhouses at Myco-Town and labs on Georgia Tech's campus.

They invite friends from the Mushroom Club of Georgia to be the first to experiment with it in their kitchens. People rave about its delicious roasted cashew flavor and a feel-good sense of well-being they get when eating it or drinking it as tea.

Ella sautés a fresh crop right now in butter with a drop of tamari and extra garlic. It's been the ideal food during pregnancy since she can feel it giving added strength and nutrients to her baby while enhancing her own mental alertness.

It sounds strange when she tries to put it into words for her girlfriend Sally. "I can distinctly sense a nurturing energy boost from inside my brain out, radiating into muscles and bones, similar to how sugars and nutrients flow through tree trunks.

"It's also a way to commune with Charlie. To bring him closer." She slips into a faraway daydream.

Ella gives a lot of thought to the new name. Since it's a completely original genus and species, the new fungus requires two names. It will be registered in international journals as *CharElla charlianii* blending both names as a symbol of their love. Its common name will be Charlie's Best.

Even with so many terrific projects soon to be launched at Myco-Town, Ella knows this is the mushroom that will be the greatest breakthrough. Charlie's Best will be the source of potent medicines and cures, delicious foods and drinks and so many other products still to be discovered.

For the first time, baby Lily starts kicking.

Chapter 19 – Lily

Little Lily's life moves 10 times around the seasons. She already speaks fluently in English, Spanish, French, Cherokee, Japanese and is learning Swahili. And she speaks the language of trees, sings the songs of birds and hears the silent growth of mushroom mycelium underfoot.

Clearly, Lily is a force. She's the next generation of *Homo splendens* with even more affinity for nature than her father Charlie. She's more than human, sensing the world from the intuitive perspectives of butterflies, tortoises, forests and clouds.

Her eyes – the color of Greek island waters – are a stunning shade of sparkling turquoise never seen before. Contrasting with her burnt sienna wavy hair, rusty-colored like chipmunks' backs and robins' breasts, she is beyond stunning.

Whenever Ella takes Lily in public, people of all ages are drawn to her, staring, marveling at her beauty. Especially small babies, unspoiled by judgment and inhibition. Their heads turn toward her from their strollers, smiling and laughing when Lily walks by. Yearning to be near her mysterious dynamism. She radiates intelligence and grace.

Lily loves music in every genre. She can hear a song once, then sing along with a perfect pitched voice that's both haunting and uplifting. Adding harmonies to John Lennon, Joni Mitchell, Bonnie Raitt, Ella Fitzgerald and Jessye Norman are one thing. But recently she starts singing along with birds, Bumble bees and frogs, adding unexpected harmonies, trills, rhythms and major and minor counterpoint melodies that are remarkable. She's building a new musical vocabulary all her own.

Ella and Grover believe Lily's rich melodies are spreading to tree communities, miles away – accelerating the growth of Georgia's remaining forests, bringing them back to recovery faster.

Back in Buckhead, tree murders are still frequent as the gnawing roar of chainsaws slash, and bulldozers scrape the soil bare to make way for concrete apartment blocks – poorly built places people will never own.

As urban wildlife habitats crumble, Ella's thickly wooded property becomes a last sanctuary inside the city limits of Atlanta, attracting birds to concentrate here, build nests, find food and shelter in the unusual trees and shrubs Grover planted long ago.

Cardinals. Chickadees. Carolina Wrens. Towhees. Nuthatches. Woodpeckers. Brown thrashers. Barred owls at night. Their songs are louder and more animated in Lily's backyard. The birds want to be where she is.

Chapter 20 – Gene

Gene Jenkins went ahead and took early retirement at 62. He couldn't stay at ChemLawn any longer. Social Security almost covers his monthly expenses.

Colon cancer saps his energy every afternoon even though debilitating chemo treatments have ended for now.

It's those weird encounters with livid animals lurching at him that affect him most, making him lethargic and desolate, searching for direction.
Maybe those damn chemicals really were a problem.
He wants his life to have a purpose but how?
That weird kid named Charlie with the long hair and piercing eyes keeps coming to mind.

Today he decides to return to Buckhead to find him.
Do I owe him an apology? Can I learn something from him? I just want to talk . . .

Gene once noticed the house Charlie walked into and thinks he remembers the street. It's the only place blanketed with mature trees planted everywhere on land that was once open lawn.

After sitting in his Jeep for a while in the cool shade of Charlie's *Sinojackia* and Silver Maple trees, Gene gets the nerve to knock on the door. Though Ella is spending most of her time at Myco-Town these days, she still returns to her city house to keep it up and visit old friends. She and Lily happen to be in town this week.

Since Ella isn't expecting anyone, she assumes it's a salesman or package delivery and doesn't intend to answer. Yet, at that moment, Charlie's voice resonates through her, coming from deep inside her spine. She can feel the warmth of his long, elegant fingers cradling her face in his hands. *It's okay, Sweetheart. Let him in. Hear what he has to say.*

Reluctantly, Ella opens the front door, trusting such a strong sign of approval.

"My name is Gene Jenkins. Doesn't Charlie live here? I met him years ago and he made a big impression on me."

Ella's face goes blank. "Charlie has been dead for 10 years."

"I'm his daughter." Lily chimes in, curious to see who's there. Her voice is full of pride and love for the father she never knew. Now, a myth.

"And I'm his partner, Ella. How can I help you, Gene?"

"I'm not sure, Ella. Gosh, I'm so sorry for your loss," he says, looking down in awkward silence.

"I know Charlie was right about a lotta things. I sprayed chemicals on lawns around here for a livin'. He said the stuff was poison and doin' real harm. No one ever questioned it before he did. I was hopin' to talk with him, to maybe learn from him. I wanted his ideas on maybe doin' things differently in my final years. I know he loved the trees and wildlife around here, and so do I . . . ."

Gene's voice trails off, heavy with sadness and uncertainty. Ella realizes he's a broken man searching for an outlet to reverse his karma.

Though it could be a mistake, she invites him in for coffee and shows him around the backyard garden. Lily joins them, feeling compassion for the wrinkled, dejected old man. He can't believe his eyes when a brown female and red male Cardinal land on the kid's head. She barely notices. They're asking Lily to make music together, but Lily would rather stay with Ella and "the new man," gently brushing the birds away until later.

Gene has never met anyone like Ella, a regal, wise young woman so connected to nature, living simply. Though it surprises them both, they enjoy each other's company, and a friendship develops when she invites him back a few more times for tea and conversation.

As she gets to know him, she realizes Gene can play a meaningful role at Myco-Town. The property needs a caretaker handyman now that construction is in full swing and several mycologists and their families are already living there. He's mentioned he and his wife are ready to get out of congested metro Atlanta. This could be the project he's looking for. If Gene and Judy Jenkins took the small cabin near the pond, he could make a meaningful contribution as a maintenance supervisor, keeping the experimental eco-village running smoothly.

"I like this idea," Gene smiles. "I could learn how to heal the Earth after a career of screwin' it up. When can we see it?"

* * *

Gene and Judy Jenkins settle into their new Myco-Town home easily. They've reinvented themselves one more time, fitting in well with the young naturalists, and bringing joy and purpose to their own lives. Gene hasn't smiled this much in years.

He proves to be a clever problem solver with roofing, plumbing, trail building and almost every practical skill that's needed. Residents appreciate and respect Gene because he makes their lives easier. In the relaxed rural environment, Gene lets his true self shine. He's nicknamed the place Shroom City.

Turns out he's a captivating storyteller, especially around the campfire, sharing tales from his boyhood growing up on a Mississippi farm where he learned to make do with "whatever resources you got."

* * *

Judy's pumpkin pie with pomegranate seeds

Judy's special talent is baking cookies and pies and Myco-T residents can't get enough. Combining homemade treats with her sunny personality, she's filling the role of a fun-loving grandmother to the youngest kids as well as their parents.

Gene, the clever and quirky granddad, has a knack for creating nature trails, something he's never done. He can visualize the best routes in his mind after studying how rains flow through the land, designing trails that curve naturally along ridges and creeks.

Lily loves the work too. She sees how Gene's trails enhance the experience of walking in the forest. She gets the other kids involved by arranging the logs he generates as edging for the paths. They stack and weave the brush he cuts into sculptural trail boundaries that double as shelter for birds and small critters. They call it Mother Nature art.

Over time, perhaps 30 years, the entire 300 acres could have a connected trail network giving easier access for mushroom hunting, exercising and taking healing breaks from computers. Ella wants to open the trails to the public a few times a year, especially when spring wildflowers peak, to engage people with Myco-Town's groundbreaking work and offer a place to recharge.

Just as Gene begins to find inner peace after his prolonged anguish, a series of dark nightmares recur that are hard to let go. They're always set at night, black and damp.

Lost in unfamiliar forests staggering alone, unable to find home.
Loud booming canons shaking the ground open.
Falling into big holes unable to climb out.
Body covered with cockroaches swarming.
Skin itching, burning, peeling away from my bones.
Stomach disintegrating from inside intestinal walls, ripping with pain.

After months of this torture, Gene confides in his wife, "Somethin's wrong with me, Judy."

She schedules a check-up with Gene's oncologist in Atlanta who hits him with the lousy news. The cancer has returned, spreading fast. They want him back on chemo. He's devastated.

* * *

Jordan Sparer, Charlie's friend and fellow scientist at Georgia Tech, moved to Myco-Town with his wife Angelina six years ago. With roots in Mississippi himself, he enjoys getting to know Gene and Judy around the late-night campfires.

One night, Judy trusts Jordan with the sad news. "I'm afraid he'll slip back into one of his deep depressions now that the damn cancer is back."

"Judy, I want to help," Jordan says. "There may be another option to chemo."

Jordan has committed the next five years to experiments blending active ingredients in Chaga and Cordyceps mushrooms to test a cancer-fighting compound he's now giving to lab mice. Early results look promising. Others have studied Cordyceps specifically for colon cancer, yet no human trials are underway. Yet as a Myco-Town scientist, Jordan has access to the unique properties of Charlie's Best. He's convinced that when used in high concentrations, this is the fungus with the greatest potential for fighting cancer.

"It's time to test my blend on a real colon cancer patient. There's nothing to lose. Do you think Gene would be willing?"

"I do. Why wouldn't he? He believes in the great work y'all are doin' here."

Based on the same concept Charlie used of blending mushrooms to increase their strength and create an instant wall to avert Gene's careless, noxious mistake, Jordan's mushroom mix – 90% Charlie's Best and 10% Cordyceps and Chaga – will enhance results that could save Gene's life. And countless lives around the globe.

Mushroom blends will become a signature of Myco-Town solutions in several disciplines.

Gene is eager to try Jordan's concoction. Fungi is dried and pulverized into fine powder steeped for hours with local honey and Passionflower vine as a soothing hot tea.

Within weeks of trying the medicinal brew, Gene gets tremendous relief right away. His energy returns. His smile is back.

After three months of daily drinks, cancer cells stop growing completely. Unlike chemo, his healthy cells are not decimated in the process, a powerful reason why mushroom therapy is so easily tolerated, boosting his immune system, and protecting the thick silver hair on his head.

Gene is among the first to be cured of cancer by the power of mushrooms, lovingly administered by a team of mycologists at Myco-Town who will transform the face of medicine because of their proprietary access to a miracle mushroom soon to be world-famous – Charlie's Best.

Chapter 21 – Growing Up in Myco-Town

Lily's ligaments and limbs stretch taller. At 12, she's already six feet two inches. Viewing the world closer to the canopy, almost from a tree's perspective. Like Jill and Charlie before her, she knows she lives life from a unique vantage point.

Ella, Lily and Grover move to Myco-Town full time. The house in Buckhead is rented to a married couple who both teach architecture at Georgia Tech and love to garden.

Grover is given a rare chance to have the experience he dreamed of – being a father from the beginning of a child's life. He eases into an unusual, cross-generational co-parenting role with Ella while sharing Lily's upbringing with the entire Myco-Town village who adores her. As the daughter of the founders, Lily is Myco-Town royalty with unlimited access to the place.

The best way Grover knows to show his love for Lily is how he showed love for Jill, planting a garden dominated by groves of trees. Always a man of few words and invisible emotions, he expresses his love through his deep knowledge of horticulture. The same way plants get better with time, so does his capacity to open his heart to his remarkable granddaughter.

One of Grover's contributions to M-Town is planting hundreds of native trees on the property in an ongoing effort that will reach full potential perhaps 100 years from now. He enlists a team of six strong mycologists; Lily is also an active member, learning together as they go. Every time a new tree goes into the ground, she presses her long fingers into the soil, bonding with the roots of the young seedling, sending love and encouragement for the mature specimen it will become.

Grover explains to Lily why he chooses each tree. "Once these Hickories and Black walnuts grow up, they'll make thousands of nuts every year as delicious food for people and animals. Over time, their thick canopies will make cooling shade," Grover tells her. "And our scientists can study which mycelium connect with which trees to trade resources and take care of each other."

"So the mycelium hold hands with the tree roots under the soil?"

"You got it, Lily. Try to imagine what that looks like."

She closes her eyes, seeing carbon, nitrogen and phosphorus transfer back and forth as sparkling, iridescent lights pulsing below her feet. She feels the heat mycelium generate as they reach out in every direction for miles, strengthening their stronghold. Holding the forest together.

*   *   *

Privately, Ella aches for Charlie every day. She could surrender to the grief and pain. Instead, she gorges on his memory for sustenance and strength, never letting go of his dreams.

She's growing into her role as Myco-Town's reigning queen, very much in charge, maturing into her own power as a respected leader and role model, inspired by Jill's journals where she learned the term Fungal Queendom.

Ella is well aware this experiment in communal living could go wrong. Failed communes of the past were run by domineering narcissists hungry for power like Jim Jones in Jonestown, Charles Manson at Spahn Ranch and Sun Myung Moon's Unification Church. Those places collapsed when members were treated like subjects, not equals. Her feminine, inclusive leadership style is more intelligent – a benevolent queen working from the same philosophy and collaborative design mycelium use.

She develops an in-depth interview process to accept new people into the community. The word is out in the tightly-knit international mycology world that securing a chance to live in Myco-Town is the place to be. At the moment, there are no openings until more housing can be built.

A rotating council of seven current residents attends every interview and advises Ella on her final decision. Lily has always been on the council too, using her unique instincts to read unseen dimensions of each candidate. Once someone passes the rigorous scrutiny, they're asked to commit to living and working here for a minimum of four years to encourage long-term involvement.

Even when accepted, not everyone makes it. A lovely Danish mycologist recommended by Professor Jakobsen at the University of Copenhagen seems eager to live here, loving the idea of getting to know like-minded Americans and their culture.

After three months, she is hopelessly homesick. Her specialized research on how mature oak roots transfer carbon through tangled fungal highways kept her outdoors too much. She can't bear the grueling hot humid Georgia summers. Reluctantly, she gives up her charming cabin for one and returns to Copenhagen, creating a rare opening on the long wait list.

A former pharmaceuticals saleswoman from the Bay Area interviewed last spring, insisting she could add value in bringing new products to market. Whenever she speaks, Lily growls, shaking her head. Ella takes Lily's reactions as a sign and denies the woman a spot. Later, they learn she was caught embezzling from her next employer and is now serving jail time.

When a scientist is accepted, their first priority is to take the lead on completing their own personal research project. They're also required to join advisory panels of two to four other research projects, plus join a group specializing in improving the property like Grover's 100-year tree planting team. Or Seattle mycologist Kate Boardman's outdoor sculpture team who works with natural elements found on the land to make art, temporary and permanent.

Living is relaxed without formal agendas or timetables, yet people remain seriously committed to their work. Every member feels the urgency for results since they're working on critical, real-world issues like finding better, cleaner solutions to avert climate change. Improve global diets. Develop organic medicines and vaccines.

Tangible outcomes from Myco-Town scientists are starting to take shape. Mycologist Duncan Ward heads the team studying effects of raw Lion's Mane mycelium taken daily in smoothies by Parkinson's patients. He's arranged a clinical trial with Emory University's Center for Movement Disorders to test and track results with 300 volunteers over five years.

Lion's Mane is the only mushroom to cross the blood-brain barrier and stimulate new neuron growth in the brain and gut. People in the study are loving the subtle effects, reporting increased energy, clearer minds, fewer tremors, and less stiffness when walking and dancing.

A genuine spirit of community is blossoming between Myco-Town families. Just like mycelium spreads to enhance relationships between fungi and trees, friendships and collaborations are linking up from the rare, shared experience of living and working together. With most of life's distractions removed, everyone realizes what a privileged situation they're building, motivating them to work harder to protect Charlie's vision.

It's the ideal environment for Lily to flourish, surrounded by nature and world-class scientists. She pops into research labs, brimming with curiosity and intelligent questions. She's a natural student, teacher and future world leader. The other children flock to her, captivated by her magnetism and startling beauty, convinced she's an enchanted princess from another planet.

They follow her around the property, climbing trees, foraging for berries and mushrooms, picking wildflowers, singing along with birds and frogs. She shows them how to make wreaths as crowns for their hair, weaving vines and grasses together with colorful wildflowers.

Lily teaches them to make intricate flower arrangements she calls Radical Ikebana, loosely based on traditional Ikebana, the centuries-old Japanese art of flower arranging.

To enliven the communal dining hall, Lily constructs complex bouquets sometimes five feet tall, contrasting and blending textures, subtle color palettes and unexpected shapes. She sees combinations no one else would consider.

One of Lily's Radical Ikebanas

Chapter 22 – Emerald Heirloom

On Lily's 13th birthday, April 22, Ella feels the time is right to introduce her precious girl to the family emerald.

"As a Taurus, emerald is your birthstone," Ella says. "And this one is extremely rare, passed down through your father's family for many generations. Now it's your turn." They place it in the center of her dresser in a carved wooden Jamaican bowl from Aunt Julie's collection. Better than any jewelry or sculpture.

Lily loves the primeval rock immediately. She visualizes how it formed over millennia to become such a substantial hunk, isolating each layer of crystal in her mind.

With a little research, Lily learns that for centuries, emeralds have been used by healers to inspire mental clarity. Emeralds are also associated with harmony, growth and abundance. A good description of the thick forests around her, breathing in emerald green life as they exhale pure oxygen.

Great grandfather Ernest liked to say, "When the student is ready, the teacher appears."

The opposite is also true. When the teacher is ready, the student appears. The wise family emerald has remained silent for 500 million years since its inception. Now that it lives with Lily every day, it's ready to communicate. But only to her; only late at night.

The extraordinary gem begins tutoring Myco-Town's exceptional nature princess. Drawing on truths developed centuries before human libraries and universities. Sometimes in words, sometimes with light patterns and vibrations only she can decipher.

Tonight, the rock passes sage intelligence from generations of Colombian rain forest healers, the country of the jewel's origin. It speaks in languages never written, only shared through spoken story.

Unlike Amazon's Alexa or Apple's Siri, this encyclopedic rock is untainted by human thought. Never limited by human imagination or technology. Its knowledge runs deeper, wider than the Nile flowing upstream. Lily's *Homo splendens* sensibility makes her one of the few who can grasp the subtle depths of its teachings.

She learns how invigorated plants feel when fresh leaves reach for sunlight every spring, nurtured from below by intricate webs of hyperactive mycelium. How infinities of ants perceive the planet from intricate nests even deeper below the soil, marching in synchronized rows, collaborating on a grand scale. How giant eagles take in panoramic vistas soaring through clouds.

Every full moon, Lily positions the jewel so silver moon beams can strike its surface. That's when its real magic turns on, lasting about five days each month during the brightest phase. She shifts its position with the seasons. Direct moonlight penetrates the jewel to coax out a delicate green light projected from its core, then shoots straight into her turquoise irises. Unexplainable life forces burst into her bloodstream.

Since many Myco-Town scientists knew Charlie personally, they speak of him often. Lily feels proud to be his daughter and yearns to know him for herself. Though her zest for life is contagious and clear, a muted melody of sadness and longing floats behind her eyes. She misses the amazing man she never met.

At night during private sessions with Emerald, she asks about Charlie and if there's a way he might speak to her from another dimension.

She's always been fascinated by early photography, especially black and white, capturing moments in history and freezing them forever. She adores photos of her parents as young children before they met, and as young lovers decades later.

"Can you make fantasy images that only exist in dreams?" she asks the sage stone.

Emerald accepts the challenge, projecting realistic images of ancient Egyptian artisans creating smooth alabaster bowls to show her how far back in history they can travel together. Tonight, as she lies in bed watching silver galaxies projected on her ceiling, a fantasy photo of Charlie holding his baby daughter close in his arms is projected into the scene. Though it never happened, it's real in this moment, giving her the comfort and connection she craves.

Then the still photo comes to life as Charlie's smile grows larger. He looks directly into her eyes and says, "I'm right here, Darling Daughter. I know you. I'm always watching how perceptive and talented you are."

She reaches her elegant arm in his direction. "I hear you, Daddy. Keep watching me."

*   *   *

Lily begins to grasp repeating patterns sprinkled across the universe.

She's already learned many human languages on her own, so Emerald enhances those lingua franca abilities, sharing late night conversations interlacing Italian with Swahili, Arabic with Cherokee.

They talk about grains of sand echoing billions of stars.
One tiny, spiraled seashell echoing spiraling galaxies.
How five-pointed starfish from California's coast recapitulate a five-petalled flower from Costa Rica. How specific formulas, different for every plant, determine how many seeds are packed into their seed pods for maximum efficiency.

At night, Rosetta Stones of shimmering white hieroglyphs twirl across every corner of her room like shadows in reverse. Though she can't grasp their meaning yet, she studies them closely hoping to understand one day. The intricate equations look like handwritten daydream doodles from personal journals of Isaac Newton or Leonardo da Vinci or great grandfather Ernest.

The stone sharpens her mind, pushing her brain to nimbly leap in any direction. Like mycelium expanding and caressing as they feed tree roots.

She becomes fluent in open-mindedness. Embraces every culture, contemporary and extinct.

There's no question she is cherished by the Myco-T community, Ella and Grover. Yet Lily grows closer to Emerald than she does to people. With no older brother, no loving father or best friend equal, the sparkling green jewel fills these empty, broken places in her heart.

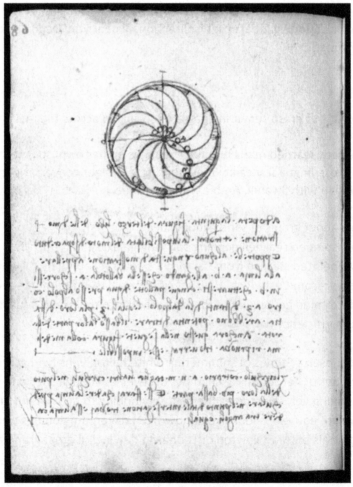

Page from da Vinci's journals often written backwards to be read in a mirror

The eager student pours her passion into loving and trusting the rock's limitless knowledge. The magnificent gem loves her right back with boundless capacity.

Their love bridges worlds of flesh and geology. Spanning centuries and stratospheres.

Lily is learning that love touches many species and comes in unlimited combinations. Love can germinate and cross-pollinate between species. And sometimes love only makes sense to the two lovers caught up in it.

Part dream, part real.
Part jagged hard like the gem, part silky soft like her flawless skin.

Lily's secret lessons will continue until she is ready to take flight.

Emerald is her first love
but it will
not
be
her
last.

Acknowledgments

Iris

Heartfelt thanks to many friends for their ongoing encouragement to complete this book, especially Bill Killen, Jemi Reis McDonald, George Skaroulis, Peter Polites, Sue Martin and Ruchi Lata Pandey.

The finished result is only possible thanks to the expert direction and wise counsel of publisher Jennifer Leigh Selig of Empress Publications.

And above all, I'm eternally grateful to Terry Grover May for teaching me to appreciate trees and plants – from learning their Latin names, to learning how to observe their subtle beauty, to recognizing their essential role in every habitat on Earth.

Photography Credits

Ella's selfie	Hannah Podhorzer
Julie and Jill	Cotten Alston
Sandhill crane	Tony Thaxton Jr
Christiana mural	Deborah Lalo
Kousa dogwood peaking	Bill Killen
Pumpkin pie	Marilyn Metzler
Author photo	George Skaroulis

All other photographs are by the author.

Author Bio

Lisa Ann Frank is a retired public relations writer who launched PR departments at the High Museum of Art and Atlanta Botanical Garden. She was director of the environment division at Turner Broadcasting where she created an award-winning commuter program encouraging mass transit, carpools and vanpools to reduce traffic and smog.

Lisa studied photography with Ansel Adams in Carmel, at Goddard College in Vermont, and the Atlanta College of Art.

Myco-Town is her first novel, set in her own extensive woodland garden in Atlanta, Georgia. Her strong environmental ethics, fascination with the natural world, and tending her wildlife and botanical sanctuary for decades are inspiration for the story.

Made in the USA
Coppell, TX
16 April 2024

31351091R00089